The Truth Behind the Lens

PAUL ANTONUCCI

PAGE PUBLISHING, INC.
New York, NY

First originally published by Page Publishing, Inc. 2019

ISBN 978-1-64544-189-2 (Paperback)
ISBN 978-1-64544-190-8 (Digital)

Printed in the United States of America

Prologue

August 17, 2001

Windows on the World 107th floor, North Tower

The elevator doors open, revealing New York's finest restaurant. Numerous light sculptures flood the hallway which lead to the main ballroom where a special ceremony is about to take place. Among the hundreds of people, stepping off the elevator is Paul Mitchell, a twenty-two-year-old employee of the United Federation for Defense of America. He's dressed in a black suit along with a long red tie and black pants. Paul was born on May 3, 1979, on Long Island to wealthy parents in Sands Point. His mother, Sabrina, is an accountant, while his father, Mark, is a high-flying businessman. Now, Paul and his parents are attending the wedding of his cousin Roy. He notices his longtime childhood friend Alyssa is their greeter for the evening.

Alyssa is twenty-six years old, has long brown hair and brown eyes, and has a nice charming smile to brighten anyone's day. She moved to Sands Point at the age of twelve, where she and Paul developed a friendship. They would hang out every weekend at his house where she became a close family friend. Now she's the greeter at the most famous restaurant in the Big Apple.

"Oh my god, Paul, it's so nice to see you again," Alyssa says, giving him a big hug.

"It's so nice to see you too. Boy, you look great," Paul says, smiling.

"Thank you. I get that a lot around here. Now, you're here for your cousin's wedding, so I'll show you to your seats," Alyssa says.

Paul looks out the many windows and sees the pink glow of the sunset light up the ballroom area.

"Wow, this place is incredible," he says.

"I'm glad you like it, but whatever job you have certainly can't be better than mine," Alyssa jokes.

"Oh, I think it is, honey. I work for the federal government," Paul says with a serious face.

"No, you don't," Alyssa says.

"Do want some ID?" Paul asks as he shows her his badge.

Alyssa is shocked and retracts her statement. "Wow, you're right, your job is better than mine. Right this way, sir," she says.

Alyssa shows them their table and hands out several menus before heading off into another room. Paul's mom Sabrina looks at him in disgust at what she just heard. "Seriously Paul, what was that?" she asks angrily.

"Relax, Mom, I'm just being myself," Paul says.

"Well, stop it," his mom whispers.

"You know what, I'm headed to the restroom," he says, clenching his teeth together.

Paul takes his time to head down a floor to the wine cellar to browse at all the fancy bottles when an employee of the restaurant John approaches him.

"There are so many bottles to choose from and so expensive," Paul says.

"Yeah, well, pick any one you want and have a seat," John says to Paul.

He walks over to the main ballroom where numerous guests talk among themselves while Alan Jenkins plays the piano in the background. Paul looks over and sees a very fit man named Matthew Pierce with his date, Anne Smith. Matt was born on March 13, 1980, in Brooklyn to an average middle-class family. His mother was an emergency room nurse while his father worked at the airport as a security guard. Tonight, he's dressed in a black suit, along with a small black bow tie, and black pants.

Paul walks over to Matt's table, the only one set up in the cellar, and sits down next to him.

"Can I help you?" he asks angrily.

"Yeah, you have to try this wine. It's fucking amazing," Paul says with joy.

"If I do, will you leave me and my date alone?" he says angrily.

"Honey, you need to calm down," Anne says. "I'm sorry, just ignore him when he does that. I'm Anne," she says, as she shakes Paul's hand.

"Fine, give me a glass," he says. Matt takes a sip and feels a rush that races through his body like a race car on a speedway. "Wow, that's incredible," Matt says. He gives some to Anne and she agrees to try some.

"That's amazing," Anne replies.

"Now, who are you, and what brings you to Windows?" Matt asks.

Paul looks out the window and sees the skyline glistening before turning back and says, "I'm Paul Mitchell. I work for the United Federation for Defense of America in DC, and my cousin Roy is getting married upstairs."

"Well, that's great news. I wish your cousin luck. As far as employment goes, I'm in the same agency," Matt says. "Matthew Pierce," he says, and they shake hands. "How come I haven't seen you around before?" Matt asks.

"I probably work in a different building. After all, it's a pretty big complex," Paul says.

"It was nice meeting you. Now, I want to finish my dinner," Matt says.

"No problem, see you around," Paul says.

They end their conversation and Paul heads back upstairs, where his mother waits impatiently.

"Where have you been, I've been looking everywhere," she says angrily.

"Relax, I was downstairs chatting with a coworker," Paul explains.

"You're not here to make friends. We're here to celebrate a wedding and have a good time," his mom says.

"I understand. I was just checking some stuff out downstairs," Paul continues to explain.

"It's about to start so take your seat," his mother says.

The pastor steps forward where Roy Harris and his soon-to-be wife, Marissa, takes each other's hands.

"Do you, Roy Harris, take Marissa Banks to be your lawfully wedded wife?" the pastor asks.

"Yes, I do," he says.

"Do you, Marissa Banks, take Roy Harris to be your lawfully wedded husband?" the pastor asks again.

"Yes, I do," she says.

"I now pronounce you husband and wife. You may kiss the bride," the pastor says.

Roy and Marissa kiss as confetti rains down from the ceiling and the live band starts playing music to celebrate the moment. Sabrina tries to hold back her tears as Paul sips his wine while enjoying the music.

He walks over to Alyssa, who's standing by the bar with several other staff members.

"Congratulations," she says, smiling.

"Thanks, you want to dance?" he asks.

"I can't, Paul. I'm working here, and besides, if the general manager sees me, I'll get fired," she explains.

"I understand, Alyssa, you have a point," he says.

"That's okay, but I'll be here if you need anything," she responds.

Back downstairs, Matt and Anne are wrapping up their date when a waiter of Italian descent checks up on them to see if everything meets their standard.

"One of the best meals we've ever had," Matt says with a smile.

"I'm glad you enjoyed it. After all, this is the most popular restaurant in the city," the waiter says with a wink. He hands him the check, and Matt can't believe how much money he will spend in one night.

"I'm literally emptying out my bank account for this," Matt says, almost choking.

"Relax, you have enough and besides, it's only a few hundred," Anne says.

"Fine," Matt says with his teeth together.

"That guy that came down here before seemed like a nice person," Anne says.

"Yeah, well I can tell they're having a good time right above our heads," Matt implies. "I'm going to let them enjoy themselves while we head out of here. Maybe I'll see that guy on Monday," Matt jokes.

Twenty-five days after the most perfect night of their lives, the towers collapsed. Nearly three thousand innocent people would lose their lives, and a nation would be forever changed. Paul's longtime friend Alyssa would be among the three thousand people killed. Paul and Matt eventually became best friends then partners for their agency. The two would end up exposing the biggest conspiracy in the world while trying to stay alive.

Chapter 1

May 2017

The sun rose over New York City, not a cloud in the sky. Driving into the Manhattan is Paul Mitchell, now thirty-eight years old. He now has a trimmed beard along with dark black hair. He's heading into the city to meet his friend Matt, whom he hasn't seen in over a decade. As he parks his car on a side street, he sees several dozen people protesting and shouting, "Our government is corrupt and needs to be exposed!"

He runs over to one of the protesters and grabs him by his collar and says, "What the fuck is your problem, man?"

"I'll tell you what my problem is"—the guy says, screaming—"our damn government needs to come clean about what happened sixteen years ago with the World Trade Center!"

"We know what happened sixteen years ago," Paul says with anger.

"I am not buying any of it. We can't trust them anymore!" the guy shouts.

"For your information, I'm an employee of your so-called corrupt government," Paul explains.

"Then you're a part of this. Get the fuck away from me!" the guy shouts again.

"You people are fucking nuts," Paul says, heading back to his car.

"Admit it, you guys are hiding something!" the guy shouts at the top of his lungs as Paul drives away.

Paul arrives at the restaurant where Matt Pierce, now age thirty-seven, waits. Matt has brown hair and a visible mustache. Just as he's about to head to the restroom, Paul walks in and high-fives his buddy and gives him a bro hug.

"Holy crap, Paul, you grew a beard," Matt says.

"You grew a mustache," Paul says back. They sit down at the table, and Paul mentions the protestors in the street. "You know, man, one of those stupid idiots outside challenged us to find evidence that our government is corrupt and hiding secrets about what happened sixteen years ago. What a piece of crap," Paul says angrily.

"Well, he has a point," Matt says.

"Are you crazy? We know what happened," Paul says. "Think about it, now's our chance to expose something huge, dude. We've been waiting a long time to do this and besides we're the only ones that can do it because we're close to the government," Matt says. "I can't believe what I'm hearing from you, man. But whatever, let's do it. But if we find nothing, I'm blaming you for wasting my time."

They throw some money on the table and leave the location.

"This could be very dangerous you know," Paul says anxiously. "No one would ever dare speak out against the government," he continues.

"You'd be surprised as to who would speak out. I guess you can say we're speaking out," Matt says. "After all, we worked for them for a long time," he continues.

"I've heard stories of people trying and never returning home, dying mysteriously," Paul says. "I don't want to join that list of people," he continues.

"Don't worry about it. We won't. Besides, we're a lot tougher than them and they didn't have government connections like we did," Matt says.

"Now where are we headed?" Paul asks.

"I know this guy named Chris, who might have what those guys are looking for," Matt explains.

"Who's Chris?" Paul asks.

"He's a radio talk show host. He does his own show about conspiracies," Matt explains. "He's been keeping a low profile and doesn't like being in public too much," he continues.

It isn't long before they come across the lone radio show host named Christopher Reed. Chris is a buff man with a very thin hairline, brown eyes and is fifty years old. Chris usually does his show in his garage and discusses a wide range of issues, from presidential elections, to conspiracy theories.

The two arrive at Chris's house, which is a white two-story split level with the garage on the side. They find him just as he's ending his radio show.

"Can I help you boys?" Chris asks in a deep voice.

"Yeah, we were told that you're the best source for conspiracy theories," Matt says to him.

"Oh, you came to the right place. What are you guys interested in knowing? I have info on Roswell, JFK, RFK, and a whole lot of other cover-ups," he says as he's showing off his collection of tapes.

"He's interested in the World Trade Center's destruction"—Paul says, pointing to his friend—"but I think its complete crap."

"It's not crap at all," Chris scowls. "I've talked to a lot of people who say things just don't make any sense about what happened," he continues. "You should rethink this. Something is very wrong," Chris says. "I should mention you guys look awfully familiar to me. Have we met before?" Chris asks.

"I don't think so. Now what do you have?" Paul asks folding his arms.

He walks over to his drawers and pulls out an old tape and wipes the dust off it. "I've been saving this for a while."

"What is it?" Paul asks.

"This is evidence of the cover-up into the towers destruction," Chris says with excitement. "It shows how they were rigged with charges by our own government," he says.

"Well, pop it in your TV and let's see it," Paul demands.

Chris pops the tape in and it shows shaky and grainy footage of a certain area of what seems to be inside the towers a few days before their destruction. An express elevator appears and three people get off and turn on their flashlights.

"This looks like complete bullshit to me," Paul says.

"Shut your mouth and keep watching," Matt says.

"I'll zoom in," Chris says. "That sure looks like foul play to me," he says, pointing to the screen.

"Do you recognize these folks?" Chris asks.

"I was going to ask you the same question," Matt says.

"Well, sadly, I don't," Chris says.

"How did you get this shit anyway?" Paul asks. "This doesn't prove a damn thing."

"Interesting story," Chris says. "I was doing my show one night, and I just went to break when my phone started ringing. I answered it, and someone in a disguised voice told me about a tape in my drawer. The guy then said that everything I needed was there. So, I went to my draw, and sure enough, I found the tape sitting there. Then I watched it and my mind was blown away."

"Is this all you have because it's really nothing," Paul says, folding his arms.

"I have two other tapes that I obtained from a source I can't reveal," Chris says. He grabs them off the shelf, makes a copy, and gives it to them. "Each tape is twenty minutes long and I have my show to get back to. Watch them, then give me a call and tell me what you think," Chris says.

"Well, you'll find out pretty soon," Matt says, nudging Paul.

They say goodbye and head toward the car. They get in the car and Paul is still frustrated at Matt.

"Great," Paul says, folding his arms.

"What's your problem?" Matt asks him.

"That's one day wasted and we only have two tapes that may contain shit," Paul says angrily.

"That's why we'll watch them and I'll tell you now they won't," Matt says convincingly.

"Well, you better show me something or else you're on your own," Paul says seriously.

"Don't worry about a thing, dude," Matt says.

The two drive away while Chris watches from his driveway squinting angrily as the car fades away into the distance.

Chapter 2

Early June 2017, 9:00 a.m.

The morning sun was hot on a late spring day in Brooklyn. Paul is up early and still annoyed that his time is being wasted. After finding nothing on the two tapes Chris gave him and his friend, he starts to think Chris is hiding something dark. Paul decides to research the conspiracy online when one article hits him in the face. The article is titled: "Journalist Found Dead after World Trade Center Explosive Residue Discovery." Paul reads the article, and it talks about how a journalist from the New Yorker was found dead in his garage from an accidental fall after finding the residue in the rubble at Ground Zero. Paul decides to call Matt, who's still sleeping.

"Hello," Matt answers.

"Dude, I found something you might want to see," Paul says.

"I thought you said I was on my own after the tapes failed," Matt says.

"Yes, but this time, I found a murder story connected to the towers," Paul says.

"I've heard about that, and no media outlet will ever report on it," Matt says, walking down stairs.

"It was written by a man named Greg Fuller of *NBC News*," Paul says.

"Go down to NBC headquarters and show it to them, then maybe they'll cover it," Matt says. Paul decides to take his friend's advice and heads down to the headquarters of NBC news to show them the article.

Paul walks in and puts the article on the desk of news reporter Tony Rao. Tony has been with NBC since the early nineties. He is tall, has black hair and blue eyes.

"What is this crap you just put on my desk?" Tony asks angrily.

"It's a story you folks in the media should be covering, instead of sitting on your ass all day," Paul says, folding his arms.

"You are an idiot, how dare you come in here and tell me how to do my job. This story is complete shit and the author of it, Greg, had to resign in disgrace from his post," Tony says in Paul's face.

"Well, sir, where can I find this Greg person?" Paul asks.

Tony shrugs and says he lives in Levittown with his wife and children. "Now get out of here and do something with your life instead of telling people how to work before I call security," Tony says, folding his arms.

Paul heads toward the door and tries to tell Tony one more time to report on his story. "Last chance, man, if I were you, I'd cover it," he says.

"Yeah, and I'll look like a complete jackass and be out of a job. Now get out of here before I call security," Tony says angrily.

Paul leaves the studio and drives away pissed off that his story won't make it to air. Paul and Matt meet again downtown.

"I showed this guy the article, and he just blew me off and said 'don't tell me how to work,'" Paul says, imitating Tony.

"Wait, he literally threatened to kick you out just because he didn't believe you?" Matt asks.

"Yes, he's a total asshole," Paul says back.

The two head into a local deli uptown and start talking about a trip to Levittown to meet with the author of the story, Greg Fuller.

"Now, you said this guy lives in Levittown, correct?" Matt asks Paul as he nods yes. "Why, you tracked him down?" he asks.

"Yep, I found out that he lives in Levittown in a two-story house, married with two children, and currently works at a bar," Matt says.

As they talk about their trip, a guy in black watches them carefully from afar trying not to be seen when a waitress approaches him. "Can I get you a drink or are you still deciding?" she asks him.

"Diet coke," the guy says in a deep voice.

"Coming right up," the waitress says.

"Think about it, bro, if this guy says his story is true, it blows the lid off of everything we know about this event," Matt tells Paul after sipping his coffee.

"Well, there's only one way to find out, and that's to get a confirmation from Greg himself," Paul says after swallowing a bite of his sandwich.

The man in black squints angrily at the two and starts snapping a series of photographs from a hidden camera in his watch.

"Well, I got his number, want me to give him call?" Matt asks.

"That's a stupid question, bro, you can't just show up at his house unexpected, he'll think we're just lost or something to that effect," Paul says.

Matt dials the number, and after a few rings, Greg answers the phone.

"Hello," he says.

"Yeah, hi, this is Matthew Pierce, I used to work for the government, and I'm interested in your story about Ground Zero," he says to him.

"Who are you, how'd you get this number, and what part of government did you come from?" Greg questions him.

"I'm from the United Federation for Defense of America, a branch of the Pentagon," he tells Greg.

"Look, I'm sick of being harassed about this story I wrote for NBC, is this a joke?" he asks angrily.

"Nope, my partner and I would like to meet with you because we read it and we believe every word of it," Matt informs Greg.

"I don't know. I guess I can squeeze in Saturday at nine o'clock if that's good for you?" Greg asks.

"Perfect, see you then," Matt says before hanging up.

"Dude, this is awesome," Paul says giving his friend a high five.

"We'll leave tomorrow morning at seven to allow for traffic," Matt says.

The two pay for their meal, then get up and leave along with the guy in black, who turns to the left as they go to the right.

Chapter 3

June 10, 2017, 7:00 a.m.

Paul and Matt prepare for the hour-long drive from the city to Levittown Long Island. The morning sun is shining on his face as Matt picks Paul up from his apartment as they start heading out for their important meeting. They encounter no traffic on the Queensboro Bridge. Paul and Matt start talking about the possibility of more stories being revealed.

"Now, this is the first story to break. Now what's the probability of more coming out?" Matt asks.

"I don't know, man, you'll have to let it play out and let it run its course," Paul says.

The two pass an intersection, and a black car turns the corner and starts to follow them closely.

"Maybe Greg has some other information he could provide us," Matt says.

"Dude, he's a former news anchor, what else could he know besides what he wrote?" Paul says.

"You'd be surprised, man, but we'll see once we arrive," Matt says.

At that moment, a gunshot destroys the back windshield of Matt's car, jolting them forward.

"What the fuck is that?" Matt says, looking behind him.

Paul turns around and sees a black car pursuing them and a guy in black firing at them. Since they used to be in government, Paul and Matt are licensed to carry firearms. Paul takes out his pistol and starts firing back when one of his bullets hits the tire of the black car forcing it off the road down an embankment exploding on impact, killing the two men inside.

"Damn it," Matt says. "What the fuck was that all about?" he continues.

"Did you notice the guy's suit and glasses?" Paul asks.

"I think so. Who was he?" Matt asks back.

"I don't know, but I saw the same guy back at the deli reading a newspaper and drinking a coke," Paul replies.

"Why would he take an interest in us? We did nothing wrong, bro," Matt says raising his voice.

"Beats me, but I think that story just might be true and that's proof of it," Paul says, putting his gun away. "If you ask me, I think we should go and report this to the police," he continues.

"I don't trust the police. I don't trust anyone out here. There's nothing we can do about them. We have a job to do," Matt says.

An hour later, they arrive at Greg's place, a two-story brown house. Matt parks in front of the house then checks his back windshield.

"Oh, my entire back windshield is gone, damn it," Matt says angrily.

"We'll worry about that later," Paul says.

"Do you know what that will cost me? I'll go broke," Matt says.

"You were in the government for a long time, bro, I'm sure you'll think of something," Paul says as he knocks on Greg's door.

The door opens up revealing Greg Fuller, age forty-two with black hair and blue eyes and a height of six foot one. "You must be Matthew," he says confidently.

"I'm Paul Mitchell. Nice to meet you, Greg," Paul says, shaking his hand.

Greg heads into the living room, where his wife and kids are waiting for him. Paul catches a glimpse of the TV which shows the accident he was just in. He nudges his friend to take a look at what's on the news.

"Is everything okay, boys?" Greg asks.

"Oh yeah, everything's fine. Let's sit down, shall we?" Matt says.

"Gentlemen, this is my wife, Kristen, and my two sons, Jimmy and Nick. Both are really good football players," he says chuckling. They walk over and shake hands before sitting down on the couch. "Now, you said you took interest in my story. Is that right?" Greg asks them.

"Yes, but why did they fire you for reporting that?" Paul asks back.

"Well, I was covering the cleanup effort in the months that followed the attack. I went to the Staten Island landfill and a guy saw what he thought was the remnant of an explosive device in the rubble. The man in charge told him not to go public with that information, but he didn't care. I heard about this guy's death one cold morning in March and I wrote it and my boss immediately asked for my resignation. He said it was a disgrace that I wrote something like this, but I know I'm right," Greg says in detail.

"I don't believe his story at all," Kristen says as she's about to sit down. "I lost a good friend in those attacks," she says, getting emotional.

"Why are these guys here?" Jimmy asks, raising his eyebrow.

"Boys, we believe something sinister is happening with your government, and your father's story just might be true," Matt says.

"If it was true, my father would still be working," Jimmy says.

"I endorse your investigation, and Kristen, stop sounding like my former boss. My story is true, and I believe more just like it will come out, you watch," Greg says, jumping off the couch. "As for you Jim, go upstairs," he tells one of his sons angrily.

"Now, do you have the article with you?" Paul asks.

"Yes," Greg says, pulling the piece of paper from his back pocket.

"Do you mind if we take it back with us?" Matt asks.

"Sure, I don't mind at all. In fact, I want my story to go public. It's about time it did," Greg says with confidence.

"Thank you for your time, sir, it's been a pleasure meeting with you and your lovely family," Paul says, shaking his hand.

"Before we head out, you have our contact info in case you have to reach us at some point later on, right?" Matt asks.

"Yes, I do, boys," Greg replies.

They exit Greg's house, and it isn't long before Matt's phone buzzes with more stories just as they hoped.

"Holy shit bro, look at this, more just broke," Matt says.

"What do they say?" Paul asks.

"One talks about a family threatened with violence if they talked about their findings. Another mentioned is a survivor committing suicide a month after escaping, and finally, a firefighter getting sick after being at the Staten Island landfill," Matt says with excitement.

"Well, a lot of firemen got sick down there from all the asbestos and shit so I'm not interested in that story because it's still happening," Paul says.

"Okay, what about the suicide story?" Matt asks.

"I don't know, it's possible the guy had post-traumatic stress syndrome and just lost his mind after being in an event that big. After all, I've had friends in the military that go through the very same thing," Paul says.

"That just leaves us with the family being threatened," Matt says.

"Now that is a story worth investigating, and I know just the man who will do just that," Paul says.

"Who are you talking about?" Matt asks.

"His name is Jacob Fields, one of Levittown's best private investigators. He has an office about a few blocks from here," Paul informs Matt.

"Well, then I guess we should pay this Jacob guy a little visit, shall we?" Matt says, grinning.

"You read my mind," Paul says.

"Let's do it," Matt says.

Paul informs Matt that Jacob has office hours from nine to six at night so the office shouldn't be crowded. He also says that you don't need to make an appointment and that he'll see them as soon as they arrive. Before they head to the office, they talk about fixing the windshield.

"Dude, we should fix your windshield before drawing any attention. I'm surprised we didn't get pulled over," Paul says.

"Good call," Matt says.

A few hours later, the two arrive at Jacob's office located in a small white building not too far from where they just left. They walk inside and approach the front desk where his secretary is busy at work.

"Can I help you gentlemen?" she kindly asks them.

"Yes, indeed you may," Paul says flirtingly. "Uh, we're here to speak with Mr. Fields," he says.

"He'll be out in about ten minutes okay, so just have a seat," she says to them.

They sit down, and Matt confronts his friend about what he said. "We're here to have a meeting, bro, not to make dates," Matt says, slapping Paul lightly across his face.

"Sorry, bro, c'mon, I was joking around," he says, trying not to laugh.

"It's not funny, man, I'm married, and I wouldn't like it if someone flirted with my wife," Matt says.

"I was married at one point too, but it ended in a divorce a while ago, so I would feel the same way, but maybe I want to start dating again," Paul says.

Jacob Fields emerges from his office, a tall man with light-gray hair and blue eyes and a very charming personality. He calls them in and sits them down and they start to talk.

"So I hear you two have a story I should look at, correct?" he asks them.

"Yes sir, indeed we do" Matt says showing him his phone.

"I reported on the story of the man committing suicide a month after his escape from the towers. He was a Levittown native, and the family was absolutely devastated. After all, the guy had post-traumatic stress. I felt horrible," Jacob says getting emotional.

"I'm sorry, sir, you must have gone through a lot," Paul says in return.

"Yeah, but I'm glad it's over and done with, I don't ever want to see that again for the rest of my career," he says angrily. "Now what's your other story?" he asks.

"It involves a family who was being harassed and threatened by the government if they exposed what they saw at Ground Zero," Matt says.

Jacob types the article name into his computer, and it pops up right away. "It says that the guy was a firefighter and his family was receiving numerous death threats and punishment if he told anyone about his findings at the site," Jacob says, reading the article. "If you ask me, I really don't believe in conspiracy theories, but this story really says a lot," he continues. "I can't say no to a story that has a ton of sources to back it up, so I'll tell you this—I'll find and call the family and ask to interview them for you and they'll provide everything they can," he continues to say.

"Thank you for your time, sir, we're glad you'll do this for us," Paul says, shaking his hand.

"I'll get back to you when my work is complete," Jacob says.

"All right, see you later," Matt says heading out the door.

The rain was coming down in buckets that night as Jacob sat in his office doing his assignment. His secretary had long since left. As he continues, the power to his office mysteriously goes out. His laptop is wireless and stays on.

"You've got to be kidding. Damn storm," he mutters.

Jacob saves his work to a flash drive before heading out to investigate the noise he just heard. He heads out into the hallway with his flashlight and sees nothing. He's the only person in the building. He turns off his flashlight and heads back to his office as the rain continues to come down heavily. Before he opens the door to his office, two men in black tackle him to the ground as they storm his office.

"Let's go, scumbag," one of the men says, escorting Jacob outside into the rain.

As one man takes Jacob away, the other takes the flash drive he left on his desk before wiping the computer hard drive clean.

"Goodbye," he says under his breath. He heads back out as the other agent approaches him.

"Go back in there and write he's taking a long-paid vacation to relieve his stress," he says.

The other agent writes the note then places it on his desk before leaving the building and disappearing into the night.

Chapter 4

June 13, 2017, 9:00 a.m.

The sun comes up the next morning, another warm summer day hits as Paul and Matt prepare to leave Levittown and head back to the city. Matt decides to head back to Jacobs' office to pick up something while Paul decides to take a day off. When Matt arrives at the office, he notices his secretary packing up early.

"I'm sorry, sir, Jacobs is not in today," she says kindly.

"What the fuck, he was just here a few days ago, where is he?" Matt asks.

"Well, when I walked in this morning, I noticed his office was empty. So, I went inside and found a note saying he's taking a paid vacation to relieve his stress," she goes on to say.

"Show me the note now," Matt demands.

She hands Matt the note and he starts to question it. "This is very suspicious to me. Did you know about this?" he asks angrily. "Look, sir, I think it's a little weird too. I mean, I tried everything. I called his cell phone, but it got sent to voice mail. Then I tried his wife and still got nothing," she says in detail.

"Son of a bitch, what happened then?" he asks.

"I don't know, sir, but we're closed until further notice," she says, heading out the door. "But here, take the note if you want," she says angrily.

"Thanks, I guess," he says.

Matt decides to take a look inside Jacobs' office. He finds nothing unusual except the door to the office is surprising unlocked.

"That's strange," he says. Matt finds the laptop computer still on the desk. He turns it on and it crashes. "What the hell?" he asks himself. "Something's wrong," he says, heading to the exit.

Matt heads back to get Paul to tell him what happened. "Dude," he says, clenching his fists.

"What, what's wrong?" Paul asks.

"I'll tell you this, our little investigative reporter took an unexpected vacation!" he says, shouting.

"You've got to be kidding me," Paul says angrily.

"Nope, I even have the note," Matt says. "I went inside his office, and his laptop was still there. I turned it on, and it didn't work," Matt says.

"They must have corrupted the hard drive," Paul says. He grabs the note out of Matt's hand then proceeds to read it. "You know what, he was definitely taken by someone. He wouldn't go anywhere without the laptop. We need to head back to the city now," Paul says, panicking.

"I agree, let's go," Matt says.

"He took a vacation to relieve his stress. Yeah, okay, that makes sense," Paul says sarcastically.

With Jacobs gone, the two have no choice but to head back to the city and start all over again. Two hours later, they arrive at Paul's apartment where they see a disk on the coffee table.

"That wasn't here when you left, right?" Matt asks.

"Nope, but let's see what this is," Paul says, putting the disk into his computer.

They hear a dark voice come through the computer speakers, "We have your little friend Jacobs. You shouldn't have hired him fellows, we're not stupid. If I were you two, I'd quit while you're ahead because we're coming for you. Don't test us, boys, we're on to your little plan to expose our secrets and we won't let that happen. You'll die before it happens. You've been warned," the voice says. Paul and Matt get chills after hearing the dark voice on the computer.

"That voice, it's so familiar to me I wish I knew who it was," Matt says.

"That's the government, man, our old agency, remember? The henchmen at the United Federation for Defense know it's us, bro," Paul says.

"I don't care about those scumbags, and we will expose every one of them," Matt says angrily.

*****

In Washington, DC, a black freight truck pulls into the garage of the United Federation for Defense, a ten-story office building near the Pentagon. The truck parks and four strongmen start unloading numerous boxes. Two of them put the boxes on a strong utility cart and proceeded to head into the freight elevator and go up to the sixth floor. They enter a huge lobby and approach the receptionist at the desk.

"Ma'am we have a delivery for Mr. Reed. He's expecting it," says one of the guys.

"I'll call his office and let him know his delivery has arrived," she says. She picks up the phone and calls Mr. Reed's office. "Sir, two men have what you've been expecting, do you want me to send them in?" she asks him.

"Yes, send them in immediately," Reed says.

"Okay, gentlemen, you can deliver the goods," she says to the two men who wait patiently. The two men wheel the cart of boxes into Mr. Reed's office.

"Sir, your packages have arrived," one man says.

The chair turns around, revealing Chris Reed, the man Paul and Matt met earlier. "Thank you, Sledge," he says deeply. "You've done good work," he goes on to say.

Sledge nods thank-you then heads out of the office as Chris opens up his packages. They contain blueprints to various buildings across America. Chris laughs silently to himself before smoking a cigar and putting his feet up on his desk.

*****

Matt decides to head back to his apartment in uptown Brooklyn, where his wife, Anne, waits impatiently. Anne is thirty-eight years old, has brown hair and green eyes, and has a height of five foot five. They married in March 2002 after dating for a full year. Anne used to work as a secretary for a prominent New York City commodities brokerage firm which lost nearly six hundred employees when the towers collapsed. She was homesick that morning and watched the events unfold on the television. Now, she's waiting for her husband to arrive home after a few days. Matt comes through the front door and Anne hugs him tightly.

"You're finally back from Levittown. How was it?" she asks after hugging him.

"Well, I came back because my little friend who I hired to investigate a story on Ground Zero ran away somewhere. Probably the government fucking around, I suppose," he says, putting his stuff down.

"Maybe you should stop investigating and start spending time with me like you did before all this even happened," she says.

"You know I can't do that, right?" Matt says.

"Yes, you can, and you will once you realize you won't like the outcome," Anne says.

"Come with me," Matt asks her.

"I can't that's not my thing," Anne says. "But I'm worried for you, something bad could happen to you or me. Think about it, sweetheart," she continues while rubbing Matt's shoulders.

Later that night, Matt has a terrible nightmare about the government taking his wife and killing her so he would keep his mouth shut. He wakes up with sweat pouring from his forehead and goes to the bathroom to wash his face when Anne hears him.

"What's wrong, honey?" she asks him.

"I just had a bad dream that's all," Matt says, drying his face.

"What happened?" she asks.

"That you get taken away and killed to shut me up," Matt says, clenching his fists.

"C'mon, honey, you know that's not going to happen. Now please come back to bed," she says to him. "Remember, it's just a dream. It's not going to happen," she continues.

"I don't want to lose you, Anne, I really don't," Matt says, trying to hold back his emotions.

"You'll forget about it in the morning," she says shutting the light off.

They go back to bed for the night, and everything calms down.

As Matt tries to get some sleep, Paul is still awake trying to catch up on his reading when the phone on his nightstand starts to ring. He picks it up and only hears someone's heavy breathing.

"Who are you, and what do you want?" he asks.

The breathing continues, which starts to get under Paul's skin.

"Asshole," he says as he hangs up.

Paul puts his book down and tries to doze off, so he shuts his desk lamp off and puts the TV on low when the phone rings again.

"Okay, listen asshole, I'm going to call the police if you call here one more time," he says angrily.

"Bro, its Matt, what's your problem?" Matt asks angrily.

"Oh, it's you. I thought it was the same douchebag prankster who called before. Anyway, what's up?" he asks.

"I can't sleep. I think they might take Anne," Matt explains.

"Why would they do that?" Paul asks.

"To shut me and you up," he continues.

"Bro, calm down, it was just a bad dream I've had plenty of them," Paul explains. "We'll talk about this later. I have to go see you later, man," he says, hanging up.

The next morning was cold and rainy and only sixty-eight degrees as Paul meets up with his buddy Matt again at his apartment for breakfast. Matt is still dealing with his recurring nightmare about his wife being taken by the government. "Dude, nothing is going to happen to Anne," Paul says.

"I hope not, bro. I've been through a lot," Matt says.

"Now, I was reading something last night before you called about a top-secret thermite lab in Washington, DC, near our old agency," Paul says.

"I've heard about that, but why wouldn't they share it with us? We've worked there for years," Matt says.

"Simple, they're afraid of whistle-blowers, and they're very good at covering their asses," Paul says raising his eyebrow. "It says it's located inside a four-story building near the Pentagon," Paul continues. "Well, we have the top-secret clearance to enter. I can't imagine why they wouldn't let us in," Matt says.

Anne walks into the kitchen and overhears the conversation about heading to DC.

"Why are you guys heading to DC?" she asks them.

"I just remembered the building contains a top-secret thermite laboratory that hasn't been disclosed to the public, and we want to check it out," Paul says to Anne.

"You guys are looking for trouble, and honey, you're over your nightmare, I guess?" Anne asks.

"I guess so, but our former agency is the one looking for trouble," Matt says, grinning.

"Okay, but you guys might not even get in there," Anne mentions.

"I have a feeling we will," Paul says, tapping Anne on her shoulder.

A few hours later, they arrive in Washington, DC, and start heading toward the building. The facility is a four-story concrete building without any windows except for the first floor where offices are located with a series of antennas on the rooftop. They arrive at a guarded entrance where Matt shows the security guard his government badge and he lets the two in.

"This is it," Matt says as they walk into the building.

The first floor is a long lobby-like area where people type away on numerous computers not wanting to be bothered.

"Everyone's so quiet," Paul whispers. "Just let them do their work," Matt says. They then head into the elevator and up to the lab. "I haven't been here in a very long time. It's like a throwback to me," Paul tells Matt. "Yeah well, welcome back I guess," Matt says sarcastically. "Don't get me started," Paul says, nudging his friend. "Now, the main scientist who runs the lab Thomas Schmidt knows me well.

He used to be an army explosives expert before he started to work in this lab," Matt informs Paul.

They get off the elevator and walk down the hallway and arrive at the lab where two huge metal doors stare at them.

"Goddamn, this has to be tighter than a bank safe," Paul says.

At that moment, the two huge metal doors start to open slowly, revealing a glamorous laboratory the size of an Olympic-sized swimming pool.

"Jesus Christ," Paul says to himself.

"Glad you like it," Thomas Schmidt says, appearing from behind a large cabinet. Thomas is a very fit individual at the age of fifty-five, has gray hair and brown eyes.

"What is this shit?" Paul says, raising his voice.

"This is one of the Defense Department's best laboratories. We have all sorts of things from viruses, to ingredients for explosives devices, and we even study human decomposition," he goes on to say. "It was commissioned by Secretary Cane in 2000 before this new guy, Newman, came in," he continues.

"Wait, Eric Newman currently serves with the new administration, doesn't he?" Paul asks.

"Yep. Why, you knew him?" Tom asks.

"No, I've heard of him," Paul says. "You're familiar with thermite, right?" Paul asks.

"Yes, I am. Now what types are you interested in, iron or copper?" he asks.

"Both," Paul says.

Thomas walks over to the cabinet in the back and takes out two huge drums filled with thermite. "This stuff will melt through any metal and won't leave a single trace behind. It can also burn while wet and can't be extinguished," Tom says.

"We believe it was used to destroy two buildings," Matt says.

"No, that's nonsense, all thermite is accounted for and closely monitored," Tom says, folding his arms. "What are you implying?" he asks.

"We're not implying anything. We're just asking questions," Paul says, stepping up close to Tom.

"This lab stays secret. I don't care if you used to work here," Tom says angrily. "The US government would never do anything sinister," Tom adds.

"Thank you for your time," Matt says as the two head out the door.

"Something's clearly not right," Paul says. "He was lying through his teeth," he continues.

*****

The two metal doors slowly shut, and Tom gets on the phone with one of the henchmen from the UFFD.

"They were just here, what should I do?" he asks.

"Destroy the lab now," a dark voice responds.

Tom then opens up one of the thermite barrels, knowing he will die anyway, then gets out the ignition powder containing aluminum and barium peroxide then sets the charge which ignites the entire barrel, creating a massive fire which sweeps the whole length of the room before exploding in a fireball.

*****

Paul and Matt get back in the car and start to head back home. As they drive down the road, the ground around them starts to shake as they hear a loud explosion behind them. Matt looks in his rearview mirror and sees the building they just exited engulfed in flames.

"Dude, what should we do?" Matt asks.

"Just keep going. We can't help those people anyway, and we don't want to get questioned," Paul says.

"I feel the heat from the fire," Matt says, starting to sweat.

"Let's get the hell out of here before the authorities arrive. We don't want to draw attention to ourselves. We're obviously on the verge of discovering something sinister," Paul says, raising his voice.

They drive away as the flames continue to intensify burning the structure. Later that evening back at Matt's apartment, he turns on the TV to channel 2 and learns more about the explosion that destroyed the building he was in earlier.

"It appears that an improper mixture of chemicals caused a massive reaction, resulting in an explosion which engulfed the entire north side of the building, government officials said in a released statement a few hours ago. As far as casualties are concerned, it appears that the building was full at the time of the explosion killing mostly everyone inside except for a few who only escaped with severe burns on their bodies. This is still an active scene, and the fire department has not ruled out foul play. Back to you in the studio," the reporter says, describing the scene.

Matt calls up Paul to see if he's watching the news, and sure enough, he is. "Bro, are you watching what I'm watching?" Matt asks.

"Yes, indeed I am," Paul replies.

"Dude, you won't believe what they say caused this," Matt says.

"What are they saying?" Paul asks.

"They're saying it was an improper mixing of chemicals—yeah, right," Matt says with sarcasm.

"What, an improper mixture of chemicals?" Paul questions. "They must think we're a bunch of dummies because we know for a fact that's not what happened at all," he continues.

"Yeah, I think we are on to something sinister here, man. It could be a lot bigger than we originally thought," Matt says.

"All right, bro, I'll see you around town," he continues as he hangs up. Paul shuts the TV off when his phone gets a message from an unknown sender.

It reads, "If you want to know more about your corrupt government and the secrets they hold. meet me at Yankee Stadium at 9:00 p.m. Come alone."

Paul reluctantly heads out to Yankee Stadium to meet this anonymous person who sent the message. He arrives at the stadium around nine and notices that it's unusually quiet, not a soul around. Paul, a little spooked by the surroundings, enters the stadium.

"Hello," he says as his voice echoes in the distance. "Anyone around?" he asks.

"Step forward," a mysterious man says stepping into view. He's dressed in a trench coat and has on a black hat.

"Who are you?" Paul asks him.

"Don't worry about my identity," the man says. "I have something very important to give you," he continues.

He then takes out a big yellow folder with the word "classified" on it written in caps then kicks it toward Paul.

"What is this?" he asks.

"Your past President James Coleman is a criminal. This guy was a complete disaster from day one. He knew he was failing, so he decided to sacrifice American lives just so he could make a name for himself. Thousands were left miserable while he and his cronies rolled around in their oil money from the Middle East," the guy says in detail.

"I don't know what to say. I mean, Coleman was a very shady individual," Paul says.

"He should be locked up for what he did," the guy says. "Inside the folder, are a series of photographs I received from a private investigator that was poisoned after he gave them to me. He said they came from a camera that was left behind in the North Tower," the guy explains. "Now, whatever you do, don't let that folder fall into the wrong hands, understand?" he says raising his voice.

"What if it does?" Paul asks.

"The consequences will be dire. I'd protect yourself, buddy, and your friends and family. Don't lose it. When the time comes, everyone will see the truth behind the lens," he says, fading into the darkness.

Chapter 5

June 23, 2017, 10:00 a.m.

Paul is nervous about this meeting. He hasn't seen Amanda Knox since he left the UFFD a while back. Amanda is thirty-eight years old, has brown hair and green eyes, and is five foot six. She used to be an intelligence officer and was Paul's former partner before he met Matt in 2001. Now, Amanda walks into the restaurant where Paul waits impatiently.

"Oh my god, Amanda, you haven't aged a bit," Paul says, hugging her.

"Thank you very much. What have you been up to recently?" she asks, sitting down.

"Well, my friend, Matt and I are exposing our government's little secrets," Paul says, sipping his water.

"Well, count me in," Amanda says. "What are you exposing?" she asks.

Paul takes out the yellow folder he received at Yankee Stadium a week ago and puts it on the table.

"Where did you get this from?" Amanda asks surprisingly.

"Some mysterious man gave it to me at Yankee Stadium a little over a week ago," Paul says.

Amanda starts looking through the folder and is shocked at what she sees. "Paul, on the night of September 10, 2001, I was summoned to building 7 at around 5:45 in the evening. I arrived at around ten to six and went up to the UFFD office on floor 23. I arrived at the office and everyone was just staring at me until I took my seat. Then a man named Chris turned around and told everyone that tomorrow would be a big day and everyone started cheering. I didn't know why everyone was cheering, it seemed odd to me. The next day, I saw it all—the smoke, the fire and the destruction. I turned on the television and heard reports of people jumping and I said to myself what have we done," Amanda says emotionally.

"Alyssa," Paul whispers to himself.

"I'm sorry?" Amanda asks.

"She was a greeter at Windows, the most famous restaurant in the city, the place where Matt and I met. She had the most beautiful smile in the world. It was the first time we'd seen each other since she took the job there, and she was a very good friend to me and my family," Paul explains, trying to hold back his emotions. "I knew she was gone as soon as the tower took its last breath. I don't know if she jumped or fell according to the reports that you heard on TV, but we miss her every day," he continues.

"Wow, that's some story. I'm sorry," Amanda says.

"It's hard to discuss sometimes," Paul says.

As the two continue their conversation, Paul notices someone staring at him from afar. He goes over to confront the man in question.

"Hey buddy, you have a problem with me?" he asks the man sitting by himself.

"No, I'm just waiting for my food to be cooked," the guy says.

"Oh yeah? Well, call off your men and leave me and my friend alone," Paul says angrily.

"I have no idea what you're talking about, sir. I don't even know who you or your friend are," the guy continues to say.

"All right, bud, you asked for it," Paul says, making a fist. As he was about to punch him, a businessman runs out of the restroom and stops Paul before he can punch him.

"What are you doing to my client?" the businessman asks.

"Wait, your client?" Paul asks confusingly.

"Yes, he's my client. We were discussing ways to improve our sales," the businessman continued.

"Oh, well I'm sorry then," Paul explains.

"Be sorry, now leave," the guy says angrily.

Paul heads back to his table as everyone stares at him in disgust.

"That was embarrassing," Amanda says, shaking her head.

"I could've sworn that that was a henchman from the UFFD," Paul says. "Now have you heard of the thermite lab in DC?" Paul asks.

"I saw that on the news about a week ago. They said it was a chemical explosion," she explains.

"Nope, I was there, and I believe that we're coming across something big. That was no chemical explosion. It was blown up on purpose," Paul explains. "Also, this folder I showed, you can't fall into the wrong hands. So, I'm putting you in charge of making sure that doesn't happen," Paul continues.

"You have my trust, but there's only one person who will take it seriously, the president of the United States, Michael Atlas," Amanda explains.

"President Atlas, huh, why would he read it?" Paul asks.

"Atlas ran on exposing government corruption. It's one of the many reasons he was elected last year," Amanda explains. "If I showed this folder to him, he'd go nuts," she continues.

"But what about former President Coleman, what happens to him?" Paul asks.

"I don't know what happens to him. You'll just have to wait," she explains.

"Estes came after Coleman left office and undid everything Coleman enacted," Paul adds.

"All right, Paul, I'll take the folder and make sure it gets to Washington, DC, okay?" Amanda says.

"Wait, before you leave, who was this Chris you spoke of earlier?" Paul asks.

"Oh, it was Christopher Reed," she explains.

Paul's jaw almost drops when he hears that name. Chris Reed, the man he and Matt met earlier, is now at the center of it all. Paul heads back to his apartment to give Matt a call.

"Bro, you're not going to believe this but Chris Reed is behind all this," Paul says, shouting.

"What the fuck?" Matt asks.

"Yeah, the radio guy we met or should I say double agent," Paul says.

"Dude, they couldn't have laid a better trap than Chris. I thought he looked familiar. We fell right into it, bro," Matt adds. "Anyway, I got a giant yellow folder from a mysterious man that contains everything we need," Paul continues.

"So, where the hell is it?" Matt asks.

"You remember Amanda, right? Well, I met with her earlier, and she told me that she'll give it to President Atlas," Paul adds.

"I don't trust her that well, man, but I still have her contact number so I'll find out myself if she's really doing that," Matt says.

"I have my confidence, you don't need to contact her at all, and you just have to wait," Paul says. "All right, but I hope you're right about her bro because if she fails, it's on you," Matt says.

As the two continue to talk, Amanda makes her way to DC to deliver the folder to the president. She starts her car and begins to drive toward her destination, the White House. While she's driving down the street, a black car with a man inside starts snapping a series of black-and-white photographs.

"Sir, she's heading toward the White House. Want me to pursue her?" the guy asks talking on his phone.

"No, just stay where you are, we'll take care of her," another guy replies.

Inside FBI headquarters, an FBI agent is being brutally beaten by one of his superiors. The agent has a bloody nose along with numerous bruise marks across his face. His superior stands over him and asks the guy a series of questions.

"What have you done with that folder?" he asks. "Not talking, huh?" He continues shoving the agent against the wall, proceeding to choke him. "Where is it?" he says again.

"I'm not telling you anything," the agent says, catching his breath.

"Let's try this again. This is a handgun. Now if you don't reveal where the folder is, I'm going to put a bullet in every part of your body," the guy says, cocking his pistol.

Before the agent can say anything, another agent enters the room. "Sir, Director Shay wants to see you," he says.

FBI director Richard Shay used to be the police chief for the state of Virginia and a former Navy SEAL before he was nominated by President Atlas to serve as FBI director. Shay has black hair, brown eyes, and has a height of six foot two. Now, he's in a boardroom with several other agents staring at a series of photographs.

"That's our woman, right?" Director Shay asks.

"Yes, it is. The UFFD says it's Amanda Knox, a former Intel officer," another agent says. "She's heading to the White House to drop off something," the agent continued. "I can't tell whether or not she has the folder," he continues.

"There's a good chance she has it. You guys know what that means?" the agent questions.

"Yes, I do. Kill her," Director Shay says folding his arms.

The agents leave the room for their assignment as Director Shay learns from the UFFD that Matthew Pierce has a wife named Anne Smith.

"So this guy Pierce has a wife, right? I think we have what we need," Shay continues.

Amanda is stopped at a red light when she notices a black car pull up behind her. The light turns green and she starts to think she's being followed. The black car bumps into the back of Amanda's car, forcing her car to turn around. Now her car faces off against one of the agent's cars.

"Not today," she says to herself stepping on the gas pedal.

"Prepare to die," the agent says, stepping on his gas pedal as the two cars head toward each other.

Amanda's car slams into the agent's car, flipping it over and turning it upside down. She then turns her car around and resumes her mission to deliver the folder to the president. The three agents come out of their car and deliver a message to their boss—"Mission failed." The message reaches Chris Reed, who sits at his desk impatiently.

"Damn it, how could those agents fail?" he asks one of his men.

"She outsmarted us," his henchman replies.

Chris slams his fist on his desk in anger. "Look, I want that folder, even if I have to pry it from their cold dead fingers," Chris says.

"Sir, we have Anne Smith. They can't say no to that," his henchman says.

"Do whatever it takes to get that folder back," Chris implies.

The henchman nods in a thank you as he leaves the room.

Matt meets Paul at his apartment so Paul can finally reveal what happened at Yankee Stadium.

"You said you got that folder from a whistle-blower, correct?" Matt asks.

"Yes, this guy laid it out perfectly for me," Paul implies. "Now, do you remember the Coleman presidency?" Paul asks.

"James Coleman was a complete disgrace. If you ask me, he should've been a one-term president," Matt says.

"It gets better, bro, because this guy told me that it was Coleman's idea to go to war in the Middle East but he had to have a catastrophic event to trigger it like the World Trade Center," Paul adds. "He also said that Coleman and his little government cronies would roll around in the dough as thousands of people bury their loved ones," Paul continues.

"Well then, that makes him a mass murderer, and he should pay for what he did," Matt says sipping his soda. "But there is a problem. Where is Coleman?" Paul asks.

"It says he's living a happy life with his wife back home in South Carolina," Matt says, looking at his phone. Their conversation gets interrupted when Matt's phone rings. It's Anne's number, but when Matt answers, he's surprised to hear someone else on the other end.

"Hello, sir, you're probably wondering why your wife isn't talking to you," the voice says.

"Who are you? Please put my wife on," Matt demands.

"Shut up and listen carefully. You have something we want, and we have something you want. Say hello, sweetheart," the guy says, giving the phone to Anne who's hysterical.

"Honey, please help me. I don't want to die. Please. Do what they say, honey, I don't want to die," she says, crying her eyes out.

"That's right, we have your sweet little wife. Now, you better call your friend Amanda and tell her to give up and to surrender, or else we're going to shoot your wife in the head. I'm loading my pistol, you have two days or she's dead," the guy says. Before the phone cuts out, Matt hears the man in charge cock his gun and hold it to Anne's forehead. "Where is it?" he asks as Anne screams in terror.

Matt, already angry, picks up his chair and throws it across the room.

"Dude, I can help you through this," Paul says getting up.

"Now they're going after my wife. I fucking knew this was going to take place. I fucking knew it," Matt says angrily. "Bro, let me help you," Paul says, repeating himself.

"No, I'm going to do this myself," Matt says.

"If I don't come back, remember me well, man," he continues.

"Of course, I will," Paul says, shaking his friends' hand as he heads out the door.

Matt races home and heads inside and notices his house was torn apart. He sees a broken window with a brick on his floor and a note on the table. It reads:

> If you want to see your wife again, come to the East River Warehouse with the folder. Come alone and don't come empty-handed or else both of you die.

Matt jumps on his motorcycle to get his wife.

As he heads out, he notices he's not alone. He sees a black freight truck turn a corner and decides to follow it.

"Where are you headed?" he whispers to himself.

His question was answered when the truck pulls into a warehouse near the East River. Matt parks his motorcycle behind a large shipping container to avoid detection. He pokes his head over to take a look and sees two guys open the back of the truck to see crates of money in the millions being unloaded. He also sees his wife tied to a metal pole with several men in the background talking. Matt waits until the men leave, then proceeds to run over to the warehouse entrance. Matt hides next to the wall then breaks the guard's neck and drags his body to the side. He walks inside and tells Anne to be quiet as he unties her from the pole as he hears the men in the background unaware of what's happening.

"Well, there it is boys, eight hundred million dollars. It took a while but it's finally here," one of them says.

"I can't believe we pulled it off," the other guy says.

"Well, all we have to do is thank former president James Coleman. Without him, this wouldn't have been possible," the main guy continues.

They pass around champagne and toast in Coleman's honor.

"To Coleman," they all say.

As Matt and Anne try to flee the scene, Anne accidentally moves a metal pipe, getting the guys attention. "Hey, get back here now!" the guy yells, taking out his gun. Matt sees a submachine gun and runs over and grabs it as Anne runs outside toward her husband's motorcycle. Matt opens fire on the three guys as he tries to escape the warehouse. He lures the three outside and continues firing as he runs toward the shipping container.

He eventually shoots and kills the three men then proceeds to kiss Anne.

"I told you I'd save you," Matt says.

"You're the best thing I could ask for," she says.

"Look, my buddy Chuck will look after you for a while. No one will screw around with an ex-Marine," Matt says. They hop on the motorcycle and head to Chuck's house in Queens.

"Who's Chuck?" Anne asks.

"We were best friends growing up, and we were college roommates for a while," Matt explains.

"Why haven't you mentioned him before? And why didn't you invite him to our wedding?" she continues to ask.

"Right after we graduated, he enlisted in the Marines and was deployed oversees almost immediately. I just heard from him recently and he can't make himself visible too much, after all, he still might be doing work for them," Matt explains.

"Anyone else I should know about?" she asks again.

"Nope, most are long gone," Matt says.

They arrive at Chuck's house at dusk where he and his guard dog, Thor, sit on the front porch. From the outside, it looks like an ordinary house except for the high security and surveillance systems that he installed. Matt parks his motorcycle in his driveway then proceeds to introduce his wife to Chuck.

"I haven't seen you in such a long time, man," Matt says, giving him a man hug. Chuck is a very buff man with tattoos on both of his arms. He has light brown hair and blue eyes and is six foot four. At age thirty-seven, he can take down almost anyone.

"I'm very glad to help you out, so this must be Anne. Don't worry about Thor, he's really well-behaved, after all, he's been to Iraq and Afghanistan with me," Chuck says in his deep voice.

"Nice to meet you, sir, you're so tall," she says.

Chuck laughs. "Thank you, I get that a lot. Now, I'll show you around."

They head inside the house where he shows them his gun collection. "I have about fifty of these bad boys. If you want, I can teach your wife how to use some," Chuck says.

"I'd like that," Anne says.

"You have nothing to worry about, ma'am. If anyone barges in here and tries to harm you, they'll have to go through me," Chuck says cracking his knuckles.

"Now who's going to watch over you?" Anne asks Matt.

"Don't worry about me, okay? I'll be fine," Matt says, hugging his wife.

"How long will I be staying here?" Anne continues to ask.

"I'm not exactly sure," Matt says.

Anne's life in now in Chuck's hands as Matt heads back to his apartment in Manhattan.

At the same time, Amanda arrives at the White House. She shows the guard at the gate her badge and is let inside. She heads inside the West Wing and is greeted by one of the president's aides.

"Ma'am what can I do for you?" the aide asks.

"Yes, my name is Amanda Knox and I have something very important to give to the president," she says.

"I know who you are—you were a former Intel officer for the Federation of Defense," the aide replies.

"I need to see him now," she demands.

"I'm sorry, I can't let you do that, besides Atlas is overseas, but I'll take the folder and give it to him when he returns," the aide says.

The aide then takes the folder and is surprised at what she sees is inside. "Oh my god," she says in shock. "Where did this come from?" she asks Amanda.

"My friend Paul said he got it from a whistle-blower in the Coleman Administration, I believe, but you shouldn't be reading that," Amanda says.

"Is the vice president here?" she asks.

"You want this to go to Tim Richards's office?" the aide asks.

Tim Richards used to teach law at Harvard before he ran for the Senate in the 1994 as a democrat. Now, he's vice president of the United States at the age of sixty-five. He has light-gray hair, brown eyes, and is five foot six.

"Yes, he is. He's got an event at the Navy yard in a little while but I'll give it to him," the aide replies.

"Make sure this folder doesn't get lost," Amanda says.

"Ma'am this is the White House. Nothing will ever get lost here," the aide says.

"Thank you very much," Amanda says, shaking the aide's hand.

Amanda returns to her home back on Long Island as night falls. She falls asleep with the TV on for a few hours until around 2:00 a.m. the next morning when she's woken up by the smell of smoke coming from outside her room. She gets up to investigate and discovers the upstairs hallway completely engulfed in flames. She heads to the window and jumps out to safety. Neighbors flood the area to assist her as one starts to call 911. Amanda stands in shock as she watches her house burn down.

Chapter 6

June 25, 2017, 2:30 a.m.

The fire sirens were screaming as they rushed to the scene. They turn the corner and see the flames soaring into the sky as the orange glow lit up the area. Emergency services follow closely behind and arrive within minutes of the phone call.

"Let's go ma'am," one of the dispatchers says, escorting Amanda off the property. She watches as firemen head inside her burning house to fight the intense fire.

A few hours later, the fire is under control. Police start to question Amanda, who's being treated in an ambulance.

"Now can you describe what happened in detail?" the cop asks.

"I was sound asleep when I awoke to the smell of smoke, and I didn't know what it was. I thought I was dreaming when I saw a wall of flame in the hallway. That's when I went to the window and jumped to safety," Amanda says in detail. As the cop writes down his information on a notepad, a fireman approaches him.

"Sir, we found a shattered glass bottle along with a broken window," he says.

"Stay here, miss," the cop says as he follows the fireman inside.

"A Molotov cocktail, we have an arson situation," the fireman says.

The cop walks back outside to deliver the news to Amanda. "Okay, ma'am, it looks like someone did this intentionally," the cop says. "Do you have any enemies that want to harm you?" he asks.

"Christopher Reed," Amanda says angrily.

"Can you describe Mr. Reed?" he asks.

"He used to be my old boss. He's very tall and buff, a very thin hairline, about middle-aged, brown eyes," she explains.

"Now where did you know him from?" he continues to ask.

"He works for the United Federation for Defense of America," Amanda explains.

"You're talking about a government official then. Why would they be after you?" he asks.

"Because I'm exposing a secret they've been keeping for years," she says emotionally. "Okay, ma'am, we have everything to build a case," the cop says.

"I'll stay with my friend Jackie for a while until I find a new place to live," Amanda says.

"We'll stay in touch," the cop replies.

Amanda then heads to her friend Jackie's house in Lynbrook. Jackie is the owner of a fashion design studio and is a 100 percent Italian. She has long black hair, brown eyes, and is five foot five and twenty-nine years old. She's known Amanda for a few years. Now, Amanda knocks on Jackie's door to see if she can move in with her for a while.

"Oh my god, Amanda, what happened to you?" Jackie asks.

"Someone burned down my house," she says, crying. "I was wondering if I can move in with you," she continues.

"Of course, you can anything for a friend," Jackie says, hugging her.

Amanda sits down on the couch when she starts to hear a series of voices in her head.

"Are you okay?" Jackie asks.

"Yes," she says, lifting her head.

"I'll go make some tea, okay," Jackie says, heading to the kitchen. Amanda starts looking at some of her friend's photos from her fashion store as she waits for her tea.

"Wow, your fashion business is really taking off," she says.

"Thank you, it ran in my family for years. I'm the new owner," Jackie says setting the tea down on the table. "Now what have you been up to recently before your house burned down?" she asks.

"I have a feeling our government is behind the fire that took my house," Amanda says, sobbing.

"That's ridiculous, no one would want to harm you," Jackie says, rubbing Amanda's back.

"The fire department found remnants of a Molotov cocktail in my living room, and I know for a fact that Chris Reed is behind this!" Amanda shouts.

"Who's Chris?" Jackie asks.

"He used to be my old boss, and now he's after me and my friends," Amanda says, burying her face in her hands.

"Amanda, what are you doing? Tell me please," Jackie demands.

"Okay, Jackie, my friends and I have evidence that my former agency is responsible for destroying the World Trade Center," she says.

"What?" she asks.

"I knew you wouldn't believe me," Amanda says.

"Amanda, I was only thirteen years old when that happened. It's seems unlikely," Jackie explains.

"Listen, Jackie, what I'm telling you is true and they're trying to silence me. It isn't long before they find where I am again," Amanda says, getting up off the couch.

"You're totally safe here," Jackie says with confidence.

Amanda starts hearing the voices in her head again, causing her to feel light-headed.

"I think you need to get some rest for a while," Jackie says. Amanda heads into one of three guest rooms and tries to rest her stress away.

Meanwhile, Paul and Matt discuss heading back to DC.

"I have a second home near Embassy Row. It's a good place to start," Matt implies.

"You know, I've been thinking about this and I just found out that Phil Adens lives around here. Maybe he has some stuff for us," Paul explains.

"I'd stay away from Phil, man. After all, the guy's a real jerk," Matt says. "When I worked with him, he betrayed me and got his ass thrown out after selling arms to terrorists," Matt continues.

"I don't care, I might pay him a visit later on," Paul says.

"Do what you want, man, but when you arrive at Phil's, you're going to regret it," Matt implies. "Anyway, I'm going to start heading down, just meet me when you're done," Matt continues.

Around dusk, Paul arrives at Phil's house just outside the city near a forest trail as someone watches through binoculars.

"Phil? Its Paul. Open up, I need to talk to you," Paul says, knocking on the door.

The door opens slightly, and Paul walks inside the house.

"Phil, where are you?" Paul asks. He walks into the kitchen and finds Phil's body on the floor along with a foamy substance in his mouth.

"Oh, my god!" Paul shouts. At that moment, a loud ticking noise grabs Paul's attention. "What the fuck is that?" he asks to himself as he investigates. He traces the noise to a closet in the next room which contains a hidden explosive device.

"Damn you, Phil," Paul says as he runs out of the house. Paul takes cover behind his car as Phil's house lights up like a Christmas tree as a massive fireball destroys the property. Paul is overcome by smoke, forcing him to head into the dense forest.

"Help!" he screams. Paul gets the attention of a few fishermen who heard the explosion. "Oh, thank God," Paul says catching his breath.

"Do you need us to call 911? You look hurt," one of the fishermen says.

"They're already coming after an event like this," Paul says.

"What the hell happened?" one fisherman asks.

"I wanted to grab some important stuff from my friend and a bomb blew his place to bits," Paul says in between breaths.

The fishermen look at the ominous cloud of black smoke that rises into the setting sky. Sirens start to blare as Paul heads back to his car to head away from the area as fast as possible. As he heads away from the scene, Matt finally arrives in DC en route to his second home. He puts on some soft music as the night settles in. He stops for a red light which takes an eternity to turn green. Finally, the light turns green and Matt gives the car some gas. As he does so, an eighteen-wheeler is going way too fast and, in a hurry, slams into Matt's car, slicing it in two, and knocking him unconscious.

The street becomes a parking lot as people jump out of their cars to help. An EMT crew arrives and pulls Matt out of the car. He's barely breathing and needs emergency surgery. They also notice the truck which has slammed into a condemned store which killed the driver. Matt is rushed into the emergency room where numerous doctors prepare for the surgery.

"This is bad," one of the doctors says.

Paul hears about the accident just before he heads on the highway. He pulls over to the side of the road and doesn't say a word. He screams at the top of his lungs as he fears that his friend might be dead. He knows it could be months before they start investigating again. It could be over forever. He would know when the time comes.

Chapter 7

August 17, 2017, 11:00 a.m.

It's the anniversary of when they first met. Never in a million years would Paul think that he'd be visiting his best friend in the hospital after surviving the unthinkable. Paul thought he'd lost him forever but he knows he fought through it. Now, as he arrives at Washington General Hospital, he's prepared to tell him some interesting news. He enters the lobby and heads into the admitting office to speak with the receptionist at the desk.

"I'm here to visit a friend. His name is Matthew Pierce," Paul says.

"He's on the third floor in room 310," the receptionist says.

Paul nods in a thank you as he heads up to the third floor. Paul enters his friend's hospital room and can't believe what he sees. His longtime friend and partner is bandaged up from head to toe after nearly being killed. He lay motionless as Paul takes a seat next to him as he begins to move his head slowly to the right.

"I'm glad you're okay, buddy," Paul says. "God was looking out for me, I guess," Matt says.

"I just can't believe a truck would just run the intersection like that," Paul implies.

"I don't know. But all I know is that one minute, I was driving and the next minute, I woke up in a recovery room," Matt explains. "I'll tell you this, my mom came here the day after and she used to work in ERs like this, but she never imagined her son almost dying in one," he continues.

"I don't know what would've happened if you didn't make it," Paul says.

"Bad things, man, bad things," Matt whispers.

"What happened to the driver of the truck?" Paul asks.

"Dead, he drove himself into a store," Matt explains.

"How convenient," Paul jokes. "Anyway, you remember when I told you I was going to visit Phil?" Paul asks.

"Yes, but I told you to stay away from him. He turned his back on you, didn't he?" Matt asks.

"Worse, he blew himself up," Paul says.

"What?" Matt asks after spitting out his orange juice. "There has to be more then that dude," Matt says.

"Okay, I went into his house and found him dead in the kitchen with a foamy substance in his mouth, then I heard a ticking noise coming from the next room, and I found an explosive device in his closet," Paul explains.

"That can only mean one thing. Phil's house was a walk-in booby trap intended to kill you and only you," Matt explains.

"I'm just glad that's over," Paul says. "But why did he kill himself then?" Paul asks.

"He probably didn't want to be interrogated by you and risk going back to prison. The guy was a scumbag, dude," Matt explains. "I don't want to talk about him anymore, okay," he continues.

"When do you think you'll be released?" Paul asks.

"The doctors said maybe a few days, maybe a week at most," Matt says. "I'll be glad to get out of here," he continues.

"I'm glad to hear that," Paul says. Paul gets a text on his phone forcing him to end his conversation. "I'm sorry I have to go. I'll see you when you get out," Paul says about to leave.

As Paul leaves the hospital, Amanda is back on her feet in NYC. She sips her coffee as she stares at the newly built skyline from a pier. The light wind blows her hair from side to side as a tall man approaches her from behind.

"Beautiful, right?" the man asks.

"Indeed, it is," Amanda replies.

"I'm James Bullock. I work as a mechanic a few blocks away," he says introducing himself.

"I'm Amanda. I'm just taking a little walk to clear my mind," she says.

"I've noticed you've taken an interest in the new skyline. Why is that?" Bullock asks.

"You know I can't tell you that," Amanda says.

"Well, say no more, because I know why. You're out to seek the truth, aren't you?" Bullock asks raising his eyebrow. "I have some info you might need," Bullock continues.

"What do you know?" Amanda asks sipping her coffee.

"Let's time travel back to September 8, 2001. I was jogging on the West Side highway, and I noticed large black trucks along with numerous strongmen carrying boxes and boxes inside the buildings. I hid behind a dumpster and took out my binoculars and saw John Coleman in a security guard uniform directing them inside. A man approached me and said the pain would be so great that I wouldn't be able to count to three if I went public," Bullock explains.

"John Coleman, the president's brother, while working as a security guard was behind all this?" Amanda asks.

"Yes, he was. I saw the whole thing," Bullock says. "Thank me later. I feel like I'm being followed. You should leave as well and go somewhere safe," he continues.

Bullock starts to sweat heavily as his breathing increases. His eyes become bloodshot as he appears to freeze in place.

"James, are you okay? You don't look so good," Amanda says, backing up.

"They're waiting for us, don't you know?" James appears to say. James then lunges toward Amanda, appearing to have lost his mind. "You won't know everything," James says, pinning Amanda to the ground.

"James, let me up. Please stop!" Amanda shouts.

James lets go of Amanda as blood drips from his mouth before he falls into the river and dies.

Amanda gets up and watches James's lifeless body float away into the Hudson.

"Oh my freaking god," Amanda says emotionally. A few hours later, she arrives at Paul's apartment.

"Amanda, what's wrong?" Paul asks.

"I don't know if I can do this much longer," she says, crying.

"What the hell happened?" Paul asks again.

"Well, I ran into this nice gentleman down by the Hudson, and he gave me some useful information about what we're trying to expose," Amanda explains.

"That's why you're upset?" Paul asks.

"No, it's what happened after. This guy just lost his mind and collapsed into the Hudson," Amanda says.

"What?" Paul asks. "Anyway, what did he say?" Paul continues to ask.

"He said that he saw Coleman's brother John helping out dozens of what appeared to be strongmen carrying boxes of what looked like explosive crates," Amanda explains.

"We're dealing with a fucking crime family then!" Paul shouts. "Amanda, keep investigating this more," he continues.

"I don't know if I can do that," Amanda says.

Paul sits down next to her. "I have faith in you. You can do this," he says.

Amanda stops sobbing as she looks Paul in the eye.

"Nothing is going to happen to you," he says.

Amanda leans forward and kisses Paul on the lips for a few seconds.

"I always thought there was a connection between us," Paul says, smiling.

Amanda laughs. "Well, I have to go," she says, getting up.

"Wait!" Paul shouts. "Move in with me," he says.

"Of course, I will," Amanda says as she opens the front door.

"I'll have something prepared for when you return," Paul hints. Amanda smiles as she heads out the door.

As the sun sets over the city, a newly married couple is partying on the yacht, *American Dream*. A friend is videotaping the entire occasion as they enter the East River. As the party continues, a warehouse explodes in a tremendous fireball. The explosion rocks the boat, knocking everyone to their feet.

"Holy shit," one of the guests says.

"I hope no one got hurt down there," another guest says.

The FDNY is alerted to the massive fire. Among the firefighters headed to the scene is fifty-three-year-old Vincent Targoda. Targoda is a battalion chief with snowy-white hair, green eyes, and is six foot one. He was the only survivor of his eight-man crew when the towers collapsed on 9/11. He never suspected anything close to a conspiracy after his traumatic experience. Now, as he heads to the warehouse fire, he is about to come face-to-face with the conspiracy himself.

The next morning, as the fire is finally under control, Paul and his friend Robert head out. Robert was a former X-ray technician and former firefighter. He's thirty-nine years old has dark brown hair, blue eyes, and is six foot one. Robert isn't a believer in conspiracies but his friend is trying to convince him otherwise. As they turn the corner, they notice the remains of a few warehouses that have burned down overnight.

"What the fuck happened there?" Rob asks.

"Let's head over there and find out," Paul says. They arrive at the warehouses where Battalion Chief Targoda stops both of them.

"I'm sorry fellows you can't enter," he says.

Paul takes out his government badge while Robert takes out his FDNY badge and Targoda lets both in.

"You have any idea what caused the fire?" Robert asks.

"This is still an active investigation, but we haven't ruled out foul play," Targoda implies.

"Were any valuables damaged?" Paul asks.

"I don't know, what are you looking for?" Targoda asks.

"Well, sir, the government used these warehouses. So it wouldn't surprise me that someone wanted to destroy them," Paul explains.

"Can you explain more?" Targoda asks.

"Well, we had information about the World Trade Center's destruction stored here, and we believe it's been destroyed in the fire," Paul explains.

"I DON'T WANT TO HEAR ABOUT THAT DISASTER EVER AGAIN!" Targoda shouts.

"Why, what happened?" Rob asks.

"Boys, sit down, I'll tell you everything," Targoda says.

"Boys, I remember that morning well, it was the most beautiful blue sky I had ever seen in my life. I was at my firehouse with my buddy Kyle. We were just talking about Monday night football while having our breakfast of scrambled eggs and bacon when we got word of a plane crash at the World Trade Center. We jumped into the fire truck, all eight of us, and headed out for our mission. We turned the corner and saw the huge hole in the side of the North Tower at about the ninety-third floor. My colleagues looked at me and told me, 'Don't be surprised if we don't come back.'

"I didn't believe him at first and I said, 'We'll put out the fire and be back before you know it.' We parked our truck under the canopy of the tower and headed into the lobby where others were waiting. As our chief was talking to another chief, we heard an explosion come from the other building, and someone shouted, 'A plane hit the second tower.' I knew right there, we were at war and this wasn't going to end well. We finally got our orders to set up a command post on the ninetieth floor so we started up the stairs to get the job done. We reached the thirty-second floor and then this loud shaking started which knocked us to our feet. The lights went out for a few seconds then came back on as we heard the radio call to abandon ship and leave. The tower next to us had collapsed to dust. I told my crew we have to leave, and Kyle looked at me and said, 'Go right ahead, but we have a job to do.'

"I doubled down on my statement and said, 'We need to leave now,' but they just started up the stairs leaving me on the thirty-second floor landing. I started heading down the stairs in a rush to get out as soon as possible. When I reached the seventh floor, I radioed to them, and all I heard was static and then one of them scream out in terror. Whatever they saw scared them to death. I finally exited the building and saw this dust on the ground that looked like a snowstorm just hit the city. But it was the remains of a 110-story building I was walking through. Everything was just so quiet I couldn't believe what I was seeing. All of a sudden, I saw this black figure land right next to me. I found out later that it was a human being who jumped from the upper floors to save him/herself. If I was standing just a few feet to my left, I wouldn't be here talking to you right now.

"It was about ten seconds later that I turned around and saw the antenna on top of the building, I just escaped from, start to fall. The noise was so loud, it was like standing next to a speeding freight train. The dust cloud engulfed me as I dove behind one of our fire trucks. About an hour later, I started walking back to my firehouse, and I was hoping they made it out of there. I knew something was very wrong when another fireman approached me and told me my crew was listed as missing. Eventually, I found out that I was the only survivor. It devastated me to a point where I fell into a deep depression for a year. But I eventually got married and had a daughter and put all this behind me. There it is boys," Targoda explains.

Paul and Rob are silent as a mouse. Rob tries his best to hold in his tears as he gets up and walks outside to get some air.

"That was a very touching story, sir. I can't believe that happened to you," Paul says.

"Thanks, now what are these documents you speak of?" Targoda asks, composing himself.

"Sir, the documents prove the government's involvement in this whole event," Paul implies.

"I can't believe you would say a thing like that!" Targoda shouts.

"Listen to me, I have evidence back home that supports what I just said. I know you want to know the truth about this whole thing, just say it," Paul implies.

"Yes, I do want the truth and nothing but the truth," Targoda says, calming down. Targoda thinks to himself for a minute about the possibility of a cover-up by the government. "Come to think about it, I witnessed suspicious activity as we were cleaning up the site," Targoda says.

"Can you be more specific?" Paul asks.

"A couple of guys in black suits and some appeared to be FBI to me," Targoda says.

"What they'd do to you?" Paul asks.

"Nothing, they just said I couldn't have access to certain areas of the site," Targoda says. "I saw them trying to cleanup everything as fast as they could and I saw one guy carrying some pieces of wire away and he just looked at me with an angry look," he continues.

Robert comes back in after pulling himself together to check up on things. "You almost ready?" he asks.

"Just about, thank you for your time sir," Paul says.

Vincent nods in a thank you as the two leave the scene.

"That was very interesting what he told us," Rob says.

"Yes, it was, bro, but when the real story comes out, everyone's going to be surprised if not upset," Paul implies.

Later on, Paul and Amanda are enjoying a nice dinner by candlelight. "In case you're wondering, I made this chicken cacciatore myself. My mother gave me the recipe," Paul says, placing it on the table.

"Wow, that's really good," Amanda says after tasting some.

"I'm glad you like it. So I guess this is our first official date?" Paul says, smiling.

"Yes, indeed. So what's been happening?" Amanda asks.

"Let's just say too much for one day," Paul says, putting his soda down. "I visited Matt a few days ago, and he said that he might be released soon," Paul explains.

"That's wonderful. He's one lucky person," Amanda says.

"Yeah, you can say that again," Paul laughs.

"Paul, when do you think this will be over?" Amanda asks.

"I don't know, until we find what we're looking for," Paul says. "You might not like what I have to say next but I'll die trying," he continues.

"I didn't like that at all and never say that again," Amanda says.

Paul sits back down as the two finish their dinner.

"That was amazing. We should do this more often," Amanda says, smiling. Paul and Amanda head into the next room where they proceed to make out on the couch.

Back in DC, an angry Chris Reed sits at his desk. He gets up and swipes everything off his desk in a fit of rage before heading to the window. His office gives him a clear view of DC as well as the White House.

"Atlas," he says clenching his teeth together.

One of his henchmen walks into the room to give him something. "Sir, I have what you want," the henchman says. "Sir, you okay?" he asks walking toward the window.

"Atlas," Chris says again with his teeth together.

"What about him, sir?" his henchman asks.

Chris turns toward him and says "I think it's time we take him out, along with the vice president," Chris says.

"I'm sorry sir, but that's too risky even for you," his aide says.

Chris shoves him against the wall and points his Glock pistol under his chin. "Do you want to spend the rest of your life in prison, do you?" Chris shouts.

"Take it easy, just put the gun down," his aide says.

"You don't get it, they need to pay," Chris shouts. He heads back to look out the window and stares at the White House, its flag waving as his henchman walks out the door.

Chapter 8

August 21, 2017, 11:00 a.m.

He couldn't wait to step outside. He's been there for the past two months, and now he's finally being released. He sits in his wheelchair as his nurse rolls him outside where his friends are waiting. Paul and Amanda step out of the car and help Matt inside.

"Good to have you back, man," Paul says.

"Thanks, I'm just glad my stay there is finally over," Matt says. "It was really lonely. As I sat there, I realized how much more I want to expose all these secrets," Matt continues.

"No one will stop us. They can try all they want, but they'll never succeed," Paul says.

"Now what's been happening, any new developments?" Matt asks.

"Yes, we ran into a firefighter after one of our warehouses containing documents mysteriously exploded. He told us his account of the day's events and it shocked us to the core. He believes something is really wrong about what happened as his access was really limited to the site by guys in black," Paul explains.

"Wow, that's really interesting. I wish I was there because if you mentioned guys in black, that means only thing—they're there to remove all evidence of wrongdoing," Matt implies.

"You want to tell him something else?" Amanda asks, chiming in.

"Spit it out, man," Matt says.

"Dude, Amanda and I are in a relationship," Paul says.

"No fucking way, man, you serious?" Matt asks.

"Yes, he is," Amanda says, smiling.

"That's great, man, congratulations," Matt says. "But where did the connection come from?" he asks.

"I was helping her out with her anxiety and we just kissed," Paul says, trying to explain. "Now all relationships aside, you better hope you don't end up back here again," Paul continues.

"Oh, don't worry about that, bro," Matt says.

"This whole thing is far from over. We still have a lot more ground to cover," Amanda says.

As Paul gets on the highway, back at the White House, President Atlas is about to hold a press conference with the Prime Minister of Britain Harry Taylor. The two are discussing everything from a recent trade deal to an antimissile system for troops in the Middle East. Even though it's the summer and congress is in recess, the president is hard at work. Among the many media outlets waiting in the rose garden, is thirty-four-year-old Rachel Chambers. Rachel, unlike other reporters, would consider herself a skeptic when it comes to government secrets. Now, as she takes her seat, the president and prime minister walk out to begin the press conference.

"I'm honored to welcome Prime Minister Taylor to the White House," the president says. "We've known each other for a long time and we just signed an arms agreement for our Middle Eastern allies to help end the war on terrorism we've been fighting for the last decade and it's time to end this war," he continues.

As Rachel listens to the president, she looks to her right and sees a man in a dark coat walk into view.

The man takes out a gun and points it at the president. Secret service agents notice the man, rush over, and tackle him to the ground while other agents take the president and prime minister inside. He managed to fire several shots, injuring a few reporters before turning the gun on himself. In the Oval Office, President Atlas and Prime Minister Taylor compose themselves as Rachel Chambers tries to catch her breath.

"I thought they were coming after me again," Rachel says.

"Relax, Rachel, no one's coming after you. You've done nothing wrong," Atlas says.

"That was crazy," Rachel says.

"You've got to a lot of crazy blokes here," Prime Minister Taylor says.

"I've dealt with worse," Atlas says.

"Mr. President, you know when it comes to government, I'm a little skeptical," Rachel says.

"A lot of my supporters are too and that's one of the many reasons I was elected," Atlas says. "You see, Rachel, I believe some forces in this city are trying to bring me down and what we just saw only proves my point," he continues. "I also have a whistle-blower who said he had info on the destruction of the Twin Towers," he continues to say.

"Are you kidding me?" Rachel asks.

"That's what one of my senior aides told me, however I have yet to see the information," the president says.

"Mr. President, if what one of your aides is saying is true, then we have some serious problems abroad," Prime Minister Taylor implies.

"I couldn't agree more, Mr. Prime Minister," Atlas says.

Paul, Matt, and Amanda arrive back in Manhattan and hear word of the shooting from channel 2 news.

"The gunman has since been identified as Jason Borden, the presidents former national security adviser. He was fired after he leaked a phone conversation involving the prime minister of Sweden and other numerous foreign policy actions with other leaders. It appears he didn't take it well and decided to kill his former boss. What a story, back to you," the reporter says.

"I can't believe this, the former national security adviser?" Matt asks, raising his eyebrow.

"This looks really suspicious to me," Paul says.

"You believe that President Atlas is a target?" Amanda asks.

"Think about it. It's not just us the federation's after. They're going after Atlas and Richards as well," Paul explains.

"Also, I gave the White House that classified folder you gave me a while back. So that makes sense when you put it together," Amanda explains.

"Now they want to take out the president and vice president?" Matt asks.

"They want that folder. I just hope it didn't fall into the wrong hands," Paul says.

"The president has confidence it won't," Amanda says.

"Well, this recent assassination attempt says we're running out of time," Matt implies.

"The federation is running out of time," Paul says angrily. "We know they're days are numbered," he continues.

At the vice president's residence, Tim Richards has been assigned the duty of looking at the contents of the classified folder from his boss. He places the folder on his desk and opens it. It reveals a plan formed by former president James Coleman with the help of the United Federation for Defense of America to stage a terrorist attack on US soil. Richards discovers the Twin Towers were the intended targets. He also reads that once the plan was executed, the money would flow into Washington, DC, in the billions.

"I can't believe what I'm reading here," Richards says to himself. "This whole thing we're doing overseas is a big joke," he continues.

He turns the page and sees a list of names of those involved. Besides President Coleman and Vice President Browning, are House Speaker Michael Corbin and other members of congress now retired or still serving. "Coleman, you're a dead son of a bitch," Richards says clenching his teeth together.

"This is far bigger then I imagined," he mutters. He turns the page again and nearly faints when he discovers past administration officials now serving alongside him and his boss.

"I need to inform Mike about this," he says rushing to the phone.

"What's going on Tim?" Atlas asks.

"I just went through that folder you put me in charge of and you better start firing a lot of people," Richards says. "A lot of people you and I work with were involved in the destruction of the Twin Towers," he continues.

"Who are they?" Atlas asks.

"DHS secretary Chris Perez, Defense secretary Eric Newman, Army secretary Dennis Bowman, CIA director Ryan Cummings, and Secretary of State Rich Abens," Richards explains.

"Those are some very serious claims Mr. Vice President," Atlas says.

"It's true, sir, fire when ready," Richards says.

"Do you know what this is going to do to my administration?" Atlas asks. "We'll be forced out," he continues. "We'll launch an investigation and we'll go from there," he continues.

"How about we just release the folder to the public? After all, you can't stand corruption," Richard says.

"We can't do that. If we release this, we'll be forced to resign," Atlas says. "Just let the investigation play out," he continues.

"Let it play out? We've been working with these people ever since they were confirmed by the Senate. I don't know how they were approved," Richards says angrily.

"Keep that folder Tim. Whatever you do, don't lose it," Atlas says.

The next morning, Paul and Amanda visit the 9/11 memorial, their first time being there since 2001. Now, as Amanda puts her hand on the memorial, she feels a rush of energy rush through her as flash images of the event begin to appear.

"Are you okay?" Paul asks.

"Yes, I'm fine, honey," Amanda replies.

The two of them sit down at a nearby table while they enjoy their morning coffee.

"You don't look well. Are you sure you're okay?" Paul asks again.

"I just have the slightest possible feeling we're in danger here," Amanda implies.

"Come on, like I said earlier, nothing is going to happen. You better get those thoughts out of your head now and fast," Paul says.

"Look, I can't help myself. How can you say we're not in danger, don't you see it?" Amanda asks angrily.

"I don't see it as much as you do. Remember, you have to be strong. Don't let them control your mind," Paul explains.

"I understand that, but you have to realize that they could be anywhere," Amanda says.

"You need to stop worrying," Paul says, sipping his coffee. "Now, anything else?" he asks.

"Are we the only ones doing all this?" Amanda asks.

"I had a feeling you'd ask about this, and the answer is no," Paul says. "Look, I have a story that Matt and I found online a couple months ago," Paul says as he takes the article out of his pocket.

"Oh my god," Amanda gasps, "Is there more just like this?" she asks.

"I don't know. That's what I'm going to find out," Paul says.

Amanda reads the article and notices something odd.

"This guy was beaten to death with a hammer honey," Amanda explains. "It says he found something called a 'red chip,'" she continues.

"Yeah, I know, unexploded material, but there's nothing we can do," Paul says.

"Yes, we can do something. Let's find out more about who else tried to expose what we're doing," Amanda says.

"Let's do it," Paul says as they get up and leave the memorial.

As they leave, a man in black reports back to his unit.

"Boss, they were just here, I'm on the move," the guy says, putting his shades down.

Back at his apartment, Matt is talking to his wife on the phone before heading out. "Yes, honey, I'm okay, you have nothing to worry about," Matt says.

"I almost lost you, and I can't go through that again," she says emotionally.

"I'm still going to do my job. Sure, I may be a little sore but that's not going to stop me," Matt explains.

"I don't know how much longer of this I can take," Anne says.

"You'll be fine, honey. I have to run. I'll talk to you later," Matt says, hanging up.

Matt jumps on his motorcycle and heads to a small building on the other side of the city where a number of people wait. Earlier that morning, Matt assembled a team of numerous researchers from all five boroughs of New York City. It's his first meeting with them in their new office. Matt arrives at the office in a small white building near the suburbs. Now, as he heads inside, he notices it's very quiet. He turns the corner and is shocked by what he sees. His team was brutally slain and beaten to death. He rushes over to one man named David who's badly injured.

"Dave, what happened? Tell me now," Matt demands.

"It…was…them," Dave says, uttering his final words.

"Goddamn it!" Matt shouts.

At that moment, he hears someone moaning from the backroom. He rushes over to find his colleague Alyssa in tears. She managed to survive the attack. "Alyssa, what the fuck happened here?" Matt asks.

"It was horrible. A bunch of guys came in here and just started stabbing everyone," she says hysterically.

"Did you recognize anybody?" Matt asks, clenching his teeth together.

"I don't know," Alyssa continues.

"Are the security cameras working?" Matt asks.

"You can check, but they probably took the tapes," she says.

"Alyssa, pull yourself together," Matt says trying to calm her down.

After a few moments, Alyssa finally pulls herself together. "What should we do?" Alyssa asks.

"I'm not sure we can trust the police," Matt says.

"We just can't leave, we have to do something!" Alyssa shouts.

"I'll think about that as I get you to a secure location," Matt says.

In the Oval Office, Vice President Richards discusses the contents of the folder with his boss in person. "Tim, as I said yesterday, we'll launch an investigation into this and see what happens," Atlas implies. "I looked into it myself, and I could find no evidence they were involved," he continues.

"They must've erased their files before their confirmation hearings," Richards says. "After all, the folder also mentioned that the defense department lost approximately 2.3 trillion dollars under Coleman," Richards continues.

"Newman wasn't in charge of the DOD at the time," Atlas says.

"Yes, that part I get, but he was involved in financing the event," Richards implies.

"Tim, we can't go public with this. Like I said, I'll look into it," Atlas says. "It's not going to happen overnight. It's going to be a while," he continues.

Vice President Richards heads back to his residence where he discovers the folder has gone missing. "No! Where is it, where is it?" Richards asks to himself. Second Lady Lisa Richards enters the room where her husband is full of anger. Lisa has short white hair, has brown eyes, and is five foot five.

"What are you looking for, honey?" she asks.

"What happened to that classified folder I read yesterday?" Richards asks.

"I have no idea. I was with you and the president earlier," Lisa says.

"That folder contained secret information about the Twin Towers' destruction," Richards says. "Damn it, someone must have taken it when we left here. It was probably one of our secret service guards," Richards continues. "I'm going to find that folder, and believe me, heads are going to roll," he continues.

Chapter 9

October 7, 2017, 5:00 p.m.

It was a warm fall evening in Sands Point, Long Island, as Paul Mitchell reconnects with his past. He's attending a party thrown by billionaire Ross Henderson, a sixty-five-year-old man with short gray hair, brown eyes, and is six foot two. He was a close friend and partner of Paul's father, Mark, during his business days and also attended the Windows on the World wedding for Paul's cousin Roy. Paul invited his friend Matt to the occasion as they sip red wine in the yard as Ross approaches both of them.

"It's good to see you again Paul, you remind me of your father," Ross says.

"Thanks. Ross, this is Matt from Manhattan," Paul says, introducing his friend.

"It's a pleasure to meet you, sir," Matt says shaking Ross's hand.

"I'm going to give you two a grand tour of my mansion if that's all right with you guys," Ross says.

"Go ahead, take us inside," Matt says.

Ross takes Paul and Matt inside his mansion where he shows them everything from his billiard room to his study lounge. Finally, he takes them upstairs to show the many guest rooms but not his room.

"Okay, guys, that's it. Now I will say that no one, and I mean no one, enters my room. If I see anyone enter, I'll have security throw them out, that includes you two," Ross says angrily. "Now, follow me back downstairs—everyone's waiting," Ross continues.

"Sure, but we're going to use the restroom first," Paul says.

"You have ten minutes. If you guys aren't downstairs, I'm coming back up," Ross says, heading to the stairs.

Matt turns around and looks at Paul square in the eyes. "It looks like your so-called friend is hiding something," Matt says.

"I've known him for years, dude, what could he be hiding?" Paul asks.

"Let's go inside his room and look around," Matt says.

"Fine, but I don't want to get thrown out of here, man," Paul says reluctantly. They enter Ross's room and start looking around to find out what he might be hiding when Matt discovers something in the bathroom medicine cabinet.

"Dude, get in here now!" Matt shouts. "Look at this, cyanide capsules," Matt says, showing Paul the bottle.

"What the fuck, where did those come from?" Paul asks.

"I don't know, man, but it doesn't look good," Matt says.

"Let's keep looking around," Paul says.

Matt puts the capsules back in the cabinet and shifts his focus to the dresser draws next to Ross's bed. Paul finds a note in the top draw from 2002.

> Ross,
>
> We're very sorry to learn about the passing of your brother Jake after his accident when he revealed his secret affair with your wife before she left you. Your wife deserves better than that horrible dirtbag and should have stayed with you. Anyway, we want to thank you for funding the biggest scheme in American history. We couldn't have done it without you. We're already receiving the money from the Middle East and it's flowing faster then a waterfall. The American people are a bunch of idiots for believing the official story. Thanks to your efforts, we're richer than ever. If I were you, I'd move out of the country where you can't be extradited. We'll even give you a list of

countries to protect yourself. We're already doing the same and we'll talk again soon

Sincerely,
The United Federation for Defense of America

Matt sees the anger building inside his friend. He knows Ross was a bad person and he was right all along. Paul's longtime billionaire friend was involved in funding the biggest event in US history.

"I can't believe this. I've known this guy for years. He worked with my father on numerous business trips and now he's a goddamn criminal!" Paul shouts.

"Calm down, man," Matt says.

"I'm not going to calm down. This is it, bro. We can't trust anyone," Paul shouts.

"Take the note with you. We better head back downstairs," Matt says as they head out of the room.

The two head back outside where Ross waits impatiently. "Where have you two been?" Ross asks, raising his voice. "I told you we were using the restroom," Matt says.

"I was born in the morning but it wasn't this morning," Ross jokes, folding his arms.

"Look, we said we were using the restroom, we're not going to say it again," Paul says angrily.

"Just know this boys—I don't like liars and I'm going to find out what you two were doing up there and if I find out you went in my room, you're going to pay big-time," Ross says, stepping up close to Paul.

"Look, it was nice seeing you again, Ross, but we have to go now," Paul says.

"Fine, see you later," Ross says.

Paul and Matt leave the party and head back to the city.

"Did you see the look on his face when we came back outside?" Matt asks.

"Indeed, bro, he knows what we're up to," Paul says. "I've known him for a long time, man. I never knew he was this corrupt," he continues.

"Well, tomorrow, let's watch him on a stakeout," Matt says.

"We can't do that and besides all he's guilty of his funding the catastrophe," Paul says.

"If he's on to us, we better watch him. He's probably destroying evidence we missed," Matt implies. "Remember, you've known him longer then I have, and I think he's guilty of more than just funding," Matt continues.

"Let's see what happens tomorrow," Paul says.

The next morning, Paul is awoken by a series of loud noises outside his apartment. He goes outside to investigate but finds nothing alarming and heads back inside. Once back inside, Paul is tackled by a masked man who holds a knife to his throat.

"You son of a bitch, you won't get away with your little plan," the masked man says.

"Not today," Paul mutters as he punches the guy in the face.

The man screams in anger before lunging at Paul trying to strangle him. Paul smashes him across the back of the head as the guy punches Paul in the gut and starts to strangle him hard. Paul takes the guy's knife and stabs him in the stomach as his grip gets lighter and lighter before he dies.

"Sleep tight, scumbag," Paul says.

Paul then proceeds to drag the body outside and places the body in the back dumpster. He then notices a red pickup truck parked across from his apartment. He searches the truck and discovers his intruder was connected to Ross Henderson.

"Ross, you're a dead man," Paul says under his breath. He heads back inside to call Matt. "Matt, get your ass down here. We're going back to Sands Point," Paul says.

Matt arrives at Paul's apartment where he sees evidence of the struggle Paul went through. "What the fuck happened in here?" Matt asks.

"It's a long story. Bro, let's launch a stakeout on Ross," Paul says. "He just sent someone to kill me," he continues.

"I told you, man, let's go," Matt says as they head to his car. Back at Sands Point, the two sit in the car and watch Ross's mansion from afar. They see him going through cabinets in his study tearing the room apart in the process.

"What the fuck is he doing?" Matt asks.

"Give me the binoculars," Paul says. "He's not doing anything now…wait…he's heading to his car…he sees us!" Paul gasps. Even though Ross is a billionaire with his own security detail, he's decided to face off against them himself.

Ross's black car slams through the gate and takes off down the street.

"Goddamn it, go after him!" Paul shouts. Ross tries to shake them off as best he could but isn't successful.

"I never thought we'd be chasing your father's business partner down the fucking streets of Sands Point!" Matt shouts back. "I told you he was hiding something!" he continues to shout.

Ross manages to run through a light before it changes, forcing Paul and Matt to stop.

"Goddamn it!" Matt shouts as he steps on the gas pedal.

"Jesus Christ, man, you're going to blow the tires off this thing if you go any faster," Paul says.

"You want to catch this guy, or don't you?" Matt asks.

"Keep going, he hasn't gotten far," Paul says. After a minute or so, they finally catch up to Ross.

"You lied to me, boys. You did go through my stuff and you know everything. I won't be captured and I won't tell you anything. I have only one thing I must do," he says to himself. Ross floors the gas pedal and crashes through a guardrail causing his car to roll down the sandy embankment landing upside down.

"Motherfucker, let's head down there now!" Paul shouts as Matt steps on the brakes. Paul and Matt slide down the embankment and find Ross's car upside down. Paul manages to pull Ross's body out of the car and finds no pulse.

"The fucker is dead," Paul says. "Now we won't know what else he did," he continues.

"Let's see if we can pry open the trunk," Matt says. The trunk opens, revealing garbage bags filled with documents. The documents revealed that Ross, along with the defense department under former president James Coleman, depleted the bank account of then Secretary Cane with the help of Defense Contractor Eric Newman, now the new secretary of defense under President Atlas.

"Newman is the current head of the DOD," Matt says.

"I don't like where this is headed," Paul says. Another document shows that Ross sent his own money, 1.2 billion dollars, to President Coleman after the event happened.

"We have to take all these documents back to the city with us," Paul says.

"Yeah, you're right about that," Matt replies.

At his private Kansas mansion, former Vice President Nick Browning sips his iced tea while sitting on his front porch when he gets an unexpected phone call.

"Sir, you better come down here," the voice says.

"What's wrong?" he asks.

"We've got three whistle-blowers who know everything about what we did regarding the Twin Towers, and they're going to expose us," the voice explains.

"I can't let that happen!" Browning shouts. "I'm not going to prison, none of us are," he continues.

"Then get your ass down here and stop them," the voice demands.

"I'll be down there in a flash, you can count on me," Browning says hanging up.

Later that night at his South Carolina mansion, former president James Coleman enjoys the late-night breeze near his swimming pool. He has light-gray hair, blue eyes, and is six foot one. When he left office in 2009, he turned fifty-eight years old. Now at sixty-six, Coleman has had some pretty serious health issues from a recent heart attack that almost killed him. He never thought that a group of whistle-blowers were about to expose his plot and believed no one ever would. Now, he's about to receive the worst news imaginable as his phone starts ringing.

"Sir, we've got a serious problem on our hands," the voice says.

"Spit it out, come on!" Coleman shouts.

"We have three whistle-blowers that know everything about our little plot," the voice says.

"You've got to be kidding me. I'm not going to rot in prison, you understand me, sir?" Coleman shouts.

"It was your idea. Now, you better come down here and fix this crap now or we all go down," the voice shouts back.

"You wait right there. We'll take care of our little whistle-blowers," Coleman says hanging up. Coleman takes his glass of water and throws it down on the concrete pavement then proceeds to shatter his glass coffee table in a fit of rage.

"Nooooo!" he shouts as his anger intensifies.

Inside, former first lady Rebecca Coleman hears her husband shouting up a storm. Now as he rushes inside, she can tell something is wrong as her husband starts showing his emotional side.

"Honey, what's wrong? Are you okay?" she asks.

"No, I've got one hell of a problem. We have three whistle-blowers that know everything that I did with my administration and they have damning evidence that they're going to reveal, which means I'm going to prison!" Coleman shouts.

Rebecca starts to cry herself which doesn't ease the mood in the room.

"Oh, pull yourself together. I'm not going to prison. I don't care how sick I am. I'm going to find those fuckers and tear them in half," Coleman continues to shout.

"Why did it have to end like this, honey, why?" Rebecca asks while she continues to cry. "You do whatever you can honey," she says starting to compose herself.

"Look at me, if I don't come back you know the answer," Coleman says.

"I don't want you to die either. We were supposed to die together at least," Rebecca says emotionally.

"If I do, I do. I lived a good life for crying out loud," Coleman says. "I have to go," he says, walking toward the exit. He approaches his escort and salutes the secret service, as if he's still president, and they pull away while Rebecca continues to sob to herself.

A few days later, Paul and Amanda continue their research into the many people that have tried to do what they're now doing. They haven't found anything in the last two months but now they feel like they found a bombshell.

"Honey, look at this," Amanda says.

"What is it?" Paul asks.

Amanda pulls several articles up on her laptop computer. "Look at this—prominent lawyer who represented WTC survivor both die in plane crash," Amanda says, reading the article title.

"What's it about?" Paul asks.

"Give me a second. Okay, it says that this guy named George Stein had damning evidence along with his client who survived the attacks and was due to show that evidence in a court hearing here in Manhattan. Unfortunately, they didn't get far because the day before they were supposed to go public, their private plane crashed into a hillside apparently caused by an engine flameout," Amanda reads.

"That guy must have been one rich son of a bitch if he was flying private planes," Paul implies.

"He and his client weren't the only ones on board. It says a number of business people also died in the crash," Amanda says.

"What's the second article you found?" Paul asks.

Amanda pulls up the second article and reads the title. "This one talks about a band of brothers fascinated with conspiracy theories most notably what we're investigating, the Twin Towers. It says they died of a murder-suicide before their house burned down," Amanda explains.

"What are the details?" Paul asks.

"It says that twin brothers Jacob and Tyler Starr were fascinated by 9/11 conspiracies most notably the Twin Towers, the JFK assassination, and the Roswell UFO crash. After their death, the media said that Tyler suffered from severe depression and lost his mind, shooting his brother in the chest. He then set the room on fire before turning the gun on himself," Amanda explains.

"What the hell kind of a story is that?" Paul asks. "Now let me get this straight. These stories received a lot of media attention and not one person raised an eyebrow at this?" Paul says.

"Apparently it appeared like a normal accident to them," Amanda says.

"Is Greg's story a hoax?" Paul asks angrily.

"No, it happened. I told you the details and the actual cause of death," Amanda says.

"Well, why the fuck didn't the same media outlets report that?" Paul asks angrily.

"They probably thought he was crazy," Amanda implies.

"It's beginning to fall into place," Paul mutters.

"What are you getting at?" Amanda asks.

"Think about it for a second. The lawyer/client, and the two brothers all were investigating the same exact thing we are, and I bet they came into possession of that classified folder you delivered, which is why they were killed in such ways we would deem mysterious like a plane crash or suicide," Paul explains.

"Interesting, I see what you mean, but all evidence they supposedly found was either destroyed or confiscated," Amanda implies.

"Maybe tiny portions, but that folder probably jumped from one person to another to another. Who knows who had it before us?" Paul explains.

"I'm going to say it fell back in the hands of the government until you received it from a whistle-blower," Amanda says. "They figured, we got rid of everyone who knows and now we have to bury the damn thing," Amanda says.

"Look, I'll be glad once this is finally released to the public, but it will come at a heavy cost," Paul implies.

"What do you mean a heavy cost?" Amanda asks curiously.

"This could jeopardize the presidency of Michael Atlas," Paul says.

"Atlas wasn't involved in this so how could this bring him down?" Amanda asks again.

"I found a shitload of documents from a friend of mine back home who was a billionaire and it says he funded the whole thing," Paul explains.

"You were friends with a billionaire who funded this?" Amanda asks.

"Let me finish. We found documents that link members of the Atlas Administration to this tragedy," Paul explains. "This was back in 2001 and they weren't working with him yet, they were just contractors for the agency they now work for," Paul continues.

"So you're saying that if this folder goes public, not only will a former president and his cronies go to prison forever but members of the current administration as well?" Amanda curiously asks.

"Remember, they were Coleman's people that were promoted to head the department so they're the same cronies you just mentioned," Paul implies.

"Well, Vice President Richards and I have been in close contact with each other ever since the president put him in charge of the folder," Amanda says.

"You haven't heard from him in a long time. What if someone took the folder right from under his nose?" Paul says anxiously.

"Vice President Richards is a very busy individual, and besides, he's next in line for the presidency. If something happens to Atlas, he's going to step up to home plate," Amanda says.

"I just hope you hear from him soon because things don't appear to make sense here," Paul says. "There's nothing we can do regarding those news articles you found. We can't reopen new case files regarding the Stein guy or the Starr brothers. We must keep researching until we find something," Paul says, looking out the window.

Later, Paul and Matt are driving down a secluded road. He doesn't know where he's going and is struck by his friend's odd behavior.

"Where are we going?" Paul asks.

Matt doesn't answer and continues driving down the road.

"You're acting really weird, do you know that?" Paul asks again.

"Be quiet and shut your mouth!" Matt shouts.

"Don't ever say that to me again! Now what the fuck is your goddamn problem?" Paul shouts back.

At that moment, Matt grabs Paul's neck really hard trying to choke him as he steps on the gas pedal.

"What the fuck are you doing?" Paul asks, trying to speak.

"What is done cannot be undone," Matt says, looking his friend in the eyes as his car plunges down an embankment exploding on impact. Paul wakes up in his bed with sweat pouring down his face. He looks to check the time and realizes it's two in the morning. He goes to the bathroom to douse his face with some cold water.

"Oh my god!" he mutters to himself. He then walks back to his bed. "What a nightmare!" he mutters again.

A few hours later, the sun rises over Washington, DC, as former president James Coleman and Vice President Browning meet for the first time since leaving office in 2009.

"It's good to finally see you again sir," Browning says.

"It's good to see too, Mr. Browning," Coleman says as they shake hands.

"Now we have to stop our three whistle-blowers and fast," Browning says.

"We all made a pledge a while back and I'm going to repeat it. We will not go to prison and we will fight every step of the way to make sure what we did never gets exposed," Coleman implies.

"Exactly, we're committed to stopping anyone who gets in our way," Browning replies

"Come with me sir, our delegates are waiting for us," Coleman says.

Coleman and Browning head to a secure facility where numerous people wait. He's gathered members from his past who helped him carry out the destruction of the towers. Among them are members of the current administration.

They walk inside and everyone erupts in applause as Coleman and Browning enter the room. "Settle down everybody," Coleman says. "We have a lot to discuss," he continues.

The conference is headed by Defense secretary Eric Newman. He turns on the monitor where it shows the people, they're after.

"These are our whistle-blowers. Paul Mitchell, Matthew Pierce, and Amanda Knox, all based in New York City," Newman explains. Their pictures show up on screen along with their home addresses. Sitting next to Newman is Department of Homeland Security secretary Chris Perez and Army secretary Dennis Bowman.

"They have what we want," Perez says. Perez is the first Hispanic cabinet secretary in US history. He's fifty years old, has a very thin hairline, has brown eyes, and is six foot two. Dennis Bowman is almost seventy years old. He used to be an Army general before receiving the rank of Army secretary. He has white hair, blue eyes and is six foot four.

"What do you suggest we do, boss?" Bowman asks, looking at Newman.

"It appears that another whistle-blower gave them a classified folder with all of our names in it. Would that person like to come forward?" Newman asks.

Everyone in the room is dead silent. No one would dare do such a thing. One person, however, seems to be a person of interest, Deputy Defense secretary Patrick Crawford.

"You seem awfully quiet, Crawford," Newman says.

"I'm fine sir, you don't have to worry," Crawford says. Pat starts sweating badly.

"I think we found our culprit," Newman says.

"What are you talking about? I did nothing wrong!" Pat shouts.

Coleman's face turns beet red with anger as he gets up and slams Pat against the wall, choking him hard. "You listen closely, you dumb bastard. We're not going to prison ever, and now you laid the groundwork for our death sentence. We have a special place for scumbags like you!" Coleman shouts in Pat's face. "This is your last chance, Pat. Are you with us or not?" Coleman continues.

"No," Pat whispers in Coleman's face.

"That's it!" Coleman shouts. He takes out a revolver and holds it to Pat's throat. "Say bye," Coleman says.

"Sir, we'll take care of him. Put the gun down," Newman says.

Crawford, at that moment, dashes out of the room toward the elevators.

"Stop him now!" Coleman shouts.

Pat gets in the elevator and the doors shut as Coleman fires his revolver at the doors. Pat runs toward the exit than proceeds to head to the White House to tender is resignation before heading to New York City. A few hours later, he arrives in New York City then heads to Paul's apartment after remembering his address. Paul is stunned when he sees a man in black on his front porch.

"I'm not here to kill the two of you, I'm here to help you," Pat says.

"Who the hell are you? What do you want from us?" Matt asks.

"I used to work for President Atlas," Pat says. "The number two at the DOD," he continues.

"I'm glad you decided to come forward," Paul says.

"You were expecting me?" he asks, raising his eyebrow.

"Someone similar, we have someone who's communicating with the vice president. He must have sent you," Paul says.

"Wrong, I sent myself. Now, I have what you want," Pat says.

"What is it?" Matt asks.

"Boys, I know that folder is in the hands of the vice president and it's about time this ends. I have people after me most notably Coleman who almost killed me," Pat explains.

"Why are you really here?" Matt asks.

"Look, I know how Coleman did what he did, and I'll explain it to you," Pat says.

"Go ahead," Paul says.

"Back in 2001, Coleman called me and one other person into his office. When we got there, he had tears streaming down his face. He said his popularity was dwindling, his supporters were leaving him, our allies abandoning us while we went isolationist. I thought he was going to commit suicide. The other guy with us had a solution, he said, 'Let's stage a terrorist attack on two landmarks.' At first, Coleman didn't buy the whole thing. Then he said, 'The Twin Towers.' We drained the DOD's bank account of billions of dollars and it was all arranged. After it all happened, he put me in charge of destroying valuable evidence. I didn't want to do it at first, but Coleman put a gun to my head and said I would die if I didn't. I heard a story that in June 2002, he killed his brother and staged it to look like a suicide while his wife buried the body. Other members involved erased their records, changed their identities, and their appearances through plastic surgery. He's nuts and must be locked up," Pat explains.

"Wow, that's a lot, sir," Matt says. "Who are you?" he asks.

"Pat Crawford, you can't give my name out," he says.

"We won't. Thank you, sir," Paul says as Crawford leaves.

"This is the biggest break yet," Matt says.

"Not really. We need to investigate this more," Paul says. Paul's receives a call from Amanda telling him to put the television on. They're stunned when they discover that former first lady Rebecca Coleman has committed suicide. Paul raises the volume to hear the story.

"Former first lady Rebecca Coleman was found dead of an apparent suicide earlier today from a self-inflicted gunshot wound to her head. We don't know why she took her own life. Investigators are still working the scene here in South Carolina. The secret service has refused to talk with reporters after learning about the suicide earlier. Condolences are flooding in from everywhere including the president and vice president, and numerous members of congress. We don't know where the former president is but a source close to us says he's attending a fund-raiser for future elections. That's all we have for now, back to you," the reporter says.

"Dude, I feel really bad right now," Paul says.

"This can only mean one thing, man," Matt says, getting up off the couch. "We're getting closer and closer to that folder being released, and the public will finally see what they've been waiting for all along," Matt continues.

"I can't believe this. I mean when a former first lady takes her own life, you might have a point," Paul says.

"We need to find out if Coleman killed his own brother, man," Matt says.

"Exactly, here's what we'll do. I found out that Coleman erected a museum after he left office in DC, and the first lady donated her diary there," Paul explains.

"We'll leave tomorrow," Matt says.

As Paul and Matt finish hearing the news of Rebecca's death, Pat Crawford loses control of his vehicle causing it to crash into a deep river, sinking and instantly killing him.

The news of Rebecca's death reaches her husband who sits in a dark room with only a small sliver of light coming through.

"My beloved Rebecca, why did it have to end like this? I feel your presence beside me. Forgive me please. Was it too much to ask? Was it me? One thing's certain, they took you from me and now they're going to pay a heavy price for what they did," Coleman says emotionally.

He starts to crumple a picture of the two of them together inside the White House before letting out a loud scream before throwing his chair against the wall.

Later, Paul's going through a box of old belongings from his past. Among the many things he finds are his high school yearbook from 1999, a football his coach gave him, and a dusty tape with his name on it.

"What the hell?" he asks to himself. He wipes the dust off and heads upstairs and pops the tape in his VCR. The tape shows grainy footage from 2003 of his former friends from high school in the forest looking for something.

"You shooting all this man?" one guy asks.

"Yes, just do your intros so we can move on already," the cameraman says.

"Hello everybody, and welcome to Conspiracy TV, I'm Zack Freidman your host, and today we're in the Pine Barrens of New Jersey trying to find one of six trucks that carried tons of gold bullion from the Twin Towers after their supposed destruction by fire. Rumor has it those trucks were abandoned with the entire gold still inside, that's why we're here," Zack says with excitement.

"Hell yeah, man," the cameraman says.

"You've got to be kidding me," Paul says in amazement.

The cameraman then turns his camera to the right, revealing Paul's former high school girlfriend Marissa Green, who's now dating Zack.

"Can we hurry this up sweetie?" Marissa asks, getting impatient.

"Follow us as we search for the abandoned trucks," Zack says.

The tape then cuts to show them apparently lost and worried. "Zack, we've been searching for hours and we have found nothing and I think we're lost," the cameraman says.

"Are you lying, honey?" Marissa asks.

"No, just follow me okay. I know where we're going," Zack says.

A wave of anxiety hits Paul in the gut as he fears what's about to happen. They finally come across an abandoned truck shrouded in trees at the bottom of a hill.

"Finally, there it is guys," Zack says.

"It smells awful," the cameraman says.

"I'm about to open the truck and we'll finally see…" Zack is shot in the head and falls backward.

"Step away now!" a voice shouts.

Marissa tries to run but is shot and killed by sniper fire. The cameraman panics and tries to run as well and manages to escape the forest before the tape cuts out. Paul is stunned by what he just saw. His former friends from high school were killed by government cronies. He starts to get worried and begins to realize that could be him in a few short months. Paul is just figuring out, they're worst days are yet to come.

Chapter 10

Late October 2017, 9:00 a.m.

The sun was shining over DC as Paul and Matt arrived at President Coleman's museum. It was built during Coleman's final year in office and officially opened the day after he left in 2009. It contains everything from his childhood, his time as a senator, then eventually president. There's even a section dedicated to former first lady Rebecca Coleman. Everyone often talks about her diary, a big red book containing several hundred pages, which no one is allowed to touch or read again, but that hasn't stopped Paul and Matt.

"Here it is, man," Matt says. "If we want to find out if Coleman killed his own brother, then we have to read Rebecca's diary," he continues.

"I'll be right with you," Paul mutters.

"Are you okay?" Matt asks.

"Not really. I just found the answer to a decade old mystery," Paul says.

"What's that?" Matt asks.

"I had three other friends that I've known since high school, Zack Friedman, Roy Chapman, and my old girlfriend Melissa Green. Apparently, I found out on a tape the real reason of their death. Matt in 2003, I received a call from Zack who asked me if I wanted to tag along with him on a mission to find a series of abandoned trucks carrying gold from the towers. I declined the offer because I didn't believe them and I thought they were crazy that they'd even believe such a thing. Dude, I was supposed to die alongside them. I was told they were mauled by animals at the funeral. The parents wanted answers but they were ignored. But now I know they were murdered by the government. Dude, I was supposed to die," Paul says, tearing up.

"Oh my god, are you serious about this?" Matt asks.

"Yes, I am," Paul says.

"If you went with them, then all this would never have happened."

"If I had gone with them and died then, yes, this would never have happened. I was supposed to be on that list of all these people that have died trying and their deaths covered up," Paul says, still tearing up.

"Look, just sitting here crying about it is only giving the government satisfaction. They want you to be this way. They want us to quit. They want us to be afraid, and we're not going to do that. Now, pull yourself together. We have a job to do," Matt says angrily.

"I agree, now let's find that diary," Paul says.

"Now you're talking," Matt says.

Paul and Matt head into the museum where they meet the curator.

"Can I help you gentlemen?" the curator asks.

"Yeah, I hear you keep the diary of Rebecca Coleman here, is that right?" Paul asks.

"Yes, we do, it's the most popular item here," the curator says.

He leads them to the first lady's section where the diary comes into focus sitting in a glass case. "Now why are the two of you interested in the diary?" the curator asks.

"I don't think you heard the news of her recent suicide?" Matt says, stepping close to him.

"Wait, Rebecca's dead?" the curator asks.

"Indeed, and we need to look at her diary because she might have destroyed evidence of a murder," Paul says.

"Get the fuck out of here now before I throw you out!" the curator shouts.

"Listen here, kiddo, we're government agents and throwing us out won't help you any and we'll be back with more. Now I suggest you cooperate or we'll arrest you for hiding evidence. Now, do we have a deal?" Matt shouts.

"Fine," the curator says.

"Here put these on so you don't leave fingerprints," he continues.

Matt opens the diary and begins reading one entry of interest. "Paul, get over here!" Matt shouts.

"What is it?" he asks.

Entry #300

Dear Diary,

It's been one full week since my husband shot my brother in law in a fit of rage at our summer home here in South Carolina. I'm starting to worry about his mental state ever since he pulled off the unthinkable last year. He's been deteriorating for a while and just recently told me that his brother would go public exposing him for what he is. He told me to dispose of the body anyway I possibly could, so I buried it in a ditch near the creek and disposed of my husband's shotgun he used to kill him. I'm starting to think James should let Browning take over control of the ship because I don't know how much longer I can take. I love being First Lady, but James is making my job harder everyday by telling me to keep quiet about my actions. The destruction of the Twin Towers he pulled off has changed him dramatically. He's ordered the destruction of evidence and has totally ruined this marriage. Popularity has consumed him and I wish he would just stop. He's not going to go to jail and neither will I.

Rebecca

"Oh my god, bro, that guy was right the whole time," Paul says.
"How can everybody be so blind to all this?" Matt asks.

"I don't know, man, but their minds are all going to change pretty quickly," Paul implies.

The curator comes back and demands the diary be put back in its case where it belongs. "Okay, guys, it's time to put it back," he says.

"Turns out we were right about Rebecca disposing of evidence in a murder her husband committed," Matt says.

"What?" the curator asks.

"You must be blind, read this!" Matt says, shoving the page in his face.

"This can't be true guys, c'mon," the curator says sweating.

"Well, it is and we need to take this back with us," Paul demands.

"I have a copy of the page you want but the diary stays here," the curator says. He gives them a copy of the page they just read and they exit the museum.

"Now we know why she committed suicide," Paul says.

"Indeed, we do, I'm stunned, man," Matt says, driving away.

Meanwhile, Amanda is back in Manhattan trying to get some rest after feeling sick the night before. As she's resting, she starts to worry that Vice President Richards isn't being truthful with her. She rushes to her phone and tries to call Richards. After a few rings, she gets one of his aides.

"Hello, I need to speak with Vice President Richards now," Amanda says.

"I'm sorry ma'am Richards isn't in right now, he's with the president at a law enforcement roundtable. Can I take a message?" the aide asks.

At that moment, Amanda collapses onto the floor and screams out in pain.

"Ma'am…hello?" the aide asks.

She wakes up a few minutes later and realizes she just had an anxiety attack. Flash images sweep her mind again but this time she doesn't see the attack but her friends in grave danger. Amanda knows they're in DC but has no way of contacting them because for some unknown reason, their cell phones have no service.

Back in DC, Coleman is still going through a period of grief. "They took my wife from me and now they're going to pay for everything!" Coleman shouts.

"She's gone sir and there's nothing you can do about it," Browning replies.

Coleman glances out the window and sees Matt's car pass by. "They're here. I recognize the vehicle," Coleman says.

"Great, you know what we need to do," Browning says.

"Yes, it's time for them to pay!" Coleman shouts as he runs out the door.

"Where are we headed?" Paul asks.

"You know that story you told earlier really told me a lot," Matt says.

"Oh, really what's that?" Paul asks.

"It means we should find those trucks and the gold they were supposedly carrying," Matt implies.

"Well, good fucking luck," Paul shouts. "That was in the New Jersey Pine Barrens over ten years ago," he continues.

"That shouldn't be a problem at all," Matt says.

A few hours later, the two are back home researching more about the gold bullion while Amanda researches more about Rebecca's destruction of evidence regarding the murder of her brother in law. Paul finds an article from the *New York Times* detailing where the gold came from and how it vanished.

"The gold was originally given to the United States as a gift from the Kingdom of Saudi Arabia whose king died of mysterious circumstances after the purchase was made," Paul reads. "The gold would be stored in a bombproof vault underneath the Twin Towers in the basement of building four," Paul continues.

"So, what about when the towers were destroyed then?" Matt asks.

"You're not going to believe this but it goes on to say that several trucks were inside the basement moving tons of the bullion away from the towers about twenty minutes before the first collapse. After the collapse, the trucks were never seen again," Paul explains. "It then says that people have reported seeing the trucks in remote areas like forests, abandoned buildings, to even the bottom of a lake," he continues.

"Your friends found one in the Pine Barrens before they were executed so why wasn't their find reported on?" Matt asks.

"It's called a cover-up dude," Paul says. "Listen to this—it also says that after the towers fell, the US government placed the blame on the Saudi government who demanded the return of all the gold they gave us," Paul continues.

"I guess that was Coleman's plan to blame an oil-rich country and then sever ties with them after a fake friendship," Matt implies. "That explains why the gold vanished, but where is it now?" Matt asks.

"It says that officials recovered one truck containing about two hundred million in gold which was given to the Federal Reserve here in the city," Paul says. "Well, there's no chance of finding it now. Most of it was found and put in high-security vaults elsewhere," Paul continues.

"Never say never, man. I believe some of those trucks are still out there somewhere, and the best place to start is the Pine Barrens," Matt implies. Paul gets hit with a wave of anxiety as he's about to head to the location where his friends were murdered, more than a decade ago, before he started his quest to find the truth. He never thought he would get this far in his investigation, but he vowed nothing would stop him or his friend from exposing the unthinkable.

Later that night, Amanda heads to her car to run an important errand for a friend. Even though New York City never sleeps, the road Amanda gets onto is surprisingly quiet with the exception of a few passing cars, maybe a truck here and there. Amanda doesn't feel like she's alone on the road as she constantly looks in her rearview mirrors only to find nothing behind her.

"Calm down, Amanda, and run the errand," she says to herself. She looks in her rearview mirror again only to see a series of bright headlights tailgating her. She steps on the gas pedal to try to get away from the unknown vehicle, but to no avail.

"I'm being followed, I'm being followed," Amanda says, panicking.

The headlights diminish and Amanda starts to calm down as she nears the exit. As she exits the highway, the sudden presence of someone following her remerges. She eventually arrives at her destination to drop off some important documents related to her cause. She takes out the documents and puts them in her bag as she walks toward the door. The door is slightly ajar, but Amanda walks in anyway.

She's horrified to discover the person whom she was supposed to hand over the documents to was hanging from a ceiling fan in his living room with the television still on but not showing anything.

"Oh my god, no!" Amanda shouts as she rushes toward the phone to try to call for help. "Hello, 911, my name is Amanda Knox and my friend just hung himself. I need help now, are you there? Hello?" she says into the phone.

She notices the line to the phone has been cut off and resorts to using her cell phone but gets no reception.

"You've got to be kidding me, no reception at all!" Amanda shouts. "This is bad," she continues. "This is only going to get worse and worse," she adds.

Realizing there's nothing she can do at the current moment, Amanda dashes toward her car and speeds away from the scene into the night as her fears mount that they can't go to anyone for help anymore, as people they trust end up dead.

The next day, Paul and Matt head deep into the Pine Barrens of New Jersey in search of one of the many trucks that were containing tons of gold bullion from beneath the towers.

"We finally made it. Now to find that truck we've been researching for the past few days," Matt says. Paul isn't that excited about finding anything as all he thinks about are his friends that died attempting the same.

"Shoot me, for God's sake, just shoot me already!" Paul screams.

"What the fuck did you just say?" Matt asks angrily. "You did not just say what I thought you just said," Matt continues.

"Yes, I said it. I want to be with them, they were my friends," Paul shouts.

Matt slaps Paul across his face. "Listen to me, if you're thinking of suicide, then I failed you as a friend. We said that we would expose the truth, not kill ourselves. It's a goddamn tape, man. I lost friends too, and I'm not a wreck. Pull yourself together, that's not going to bring them back. We have a job to do," Matt explains.

"Forgive me, please. I'm sorry for that," Paul says remorsefully.

"I forgive you, man, but don't ever say that again," Matt says. "Look, when my father died a few years ago, I went through the exact same thing, but I got over it and I'm still living my life until it's my time," Matt continues.

"I'm sorry to hear that, bro. You're right, we have a job to do," Paul says, composing himself.

"There you go. Now come on," Matt says.

"How far do we have to walk to find this? It's possible it could be gone," Paul says.

"As far as it takes, and I think we'll find something," Matt implies.

"I don't want to be out here all day," Paul says.

"If we are, who cares at this point," Matt says.

"I just hope Amanda's all right. Even though we're investigating at the same time, I'm still worried about her," Paul says anxiously.

"I'm sure she's fine, and besides we'll check on each other soon," Matt explains. Paul and Matt eventually reach the top of a small hill, where they each take out a pair of binoculars.

Paul looks to the left and Matt looks to the right. They seem to see nothing except miles and miles of trees until Matt looks straight ahead.

"Look over there in the distance," Matt says, putting his binoculars down. "Is that what I think it is?" Matt asks, looking at Paul.

Paul looks in the same direction and sees a black truck in the distance shrouded in the trees that surround them.

"There it is, man. I had a feeling it would still be there," Matt says with excitement.

"Holy shit, you were right, man. It is still there," Paul says, still nervous. "It's the same truck from the video," Paul continues.

"Well, let's head down there and see if it's carrying that gold," Matt says.

A few minutes later, they arrive at the abandoned black truck rumored to be carrying hundreds of gold bullion bars from the towers.

"It's untouched," Matt says.

"Don't get too close, it could be a trap," Paul explains.

"Hey, look at this, its tires are flat, all eighteen," Matt says.

"There's also plant life coming in through the seats and flooring too," Paul implies.

"All right, let's open this sucker up," Matt says.

"I can't look, man," Paul says anxiously. "I'm afraid you're going to get shot," he continues.

"Stop thinking that. Nothing's going to happen to us," Matt says.

Matt opens up the back of the truck as an acrid stench fills the air.

"Oh my god that's horrible, what is that?" Paul asks, backing away.

"I don't know. I think it's the remnants of that tragic day," Matt explains. "Give me your flashlight!" Matt shouts.

Paul tosses Matt his flashlight and he shines it into the truck. He's stunned to see stacks and stacks of gold bullion bars each about a couple hundred thousand dollars per bar. Paul walks over and nearly faints.

"I can't believe what I'm seeing here," Paul says.

"Get as many photos as you'd like, man," Matt says, stepping out.

"You're covered in dust, man, holy shit," Paul says.

"I'm going to throw these clothes out after this," Matt says.

Paul snaps a series of photos before they decide to leave the area.

"Do you know where we are at this point?" Paul asks.

"We'll go in the direction we came. I'm very glad we found this, and see, I'm still alive," Matt says.

"Well, you got lucky, I guess," Paul says. "Wait, the tires on this truck were perfectly fine in the tape I saw," Paul continues.

"Well, that means someone planned to drive it away from here but got stopped when they discovered the slashed tires," Matt implies.

"We can't just remove every gold bar in this truck. It's best if it stays here, I hate to say," Paul says.

"Agreed, but we have photographic evidence of this now so that's even better," Matt says.

"I think we better head out of here fast before something happens," Paul says.

"Let's go," Matt says.

Later in DC, a team of SWAT officers breach an abandoned warehouse near the Ronald Reagan Washington National Airport. Inside are more than a dozen masked men with assault rifles armed and ready for a fight. They knew they'd be captured eventually. The masked men exchange gunfire with numerous armored officers as they take cover behind a series of large crates. The armored officers managed to kill every single masked man before searching the warehouse.

"We've got them, it's all clear!" the main officer in charge yells.

As one officer checks out the back of the warehouse, he stumbles across the classified folder stolen from the vice president's residence a while back.

"I've got it," he radios.

At that moment, another team of officers arrive with the vice president behind them. The officer inside the warehouse walks out to hand Richards the folder that he's been looking for.

"Good work men," Richards says.

"They're all neutralized sir," the officer says.

Richards walks into the warehouse where he sees one of the many deceased masked individuals and pulls off the mask of one person. He recognizes the face, a member of his secret service detail. Richards shakes his head in disgust before turning back to the officer in charge.

"Get them out of here," Richards says.

"Who are the others, sir?" the officer asks. "You've seemed to have taken an interest in this man," he continues.

"He used to work for me. After all, he protected me then betrayed me," Richards implies. "As for the others, I don't know. You figure that one out," he continues.

The vice president proceeds to walk out of the warehouse to let the other officers on the scene do their job. He then is escorted by other secret service agents back to his motorcade where he heads back to his residence. On the way, he looks at the folder and has just about had it.

"I lost you and now I believe it's time to make you public," Richards mutters to himself.

Back in the Pine Barrens, Paul and Matt's excitement after discovering the long-lost gold from the towers is cut short when Paul hears a familiar sound, a gunshot coming from the distance.

"What the hell was that?" Paul asks as he and Matt both take out their firearms.

"It sounded like a gunshot," Matt says.

"That's what it was. I had a feeling someone was out here with us, I knew it!" Paul shouts.

"Stay calm, and be alert," Matt says. They both hear the noise again along with someone shouting at them.

"Stop now!" the voice shouts.

Paul points his firearm in the voice's direction. "Show yourself now," Paul shouts back.

"I think it's best if we head out of here," Matt says.

The two start running with their firearms by their sides as they make it toward the dirt road they entered on.

"The car is this way!" Matt shouts. They eventually find the car as they're knocked to the floor by an explosion. "What the hell now?" Matt asks as they get into the car.

"There's a small bridge not too far from here. We'll see when we get there," Paul says.

They get to the bridge which offers startling views of the surrounding forest from left to right as well as a large body of water. The two get to the bridge and leave the car. What they see is stunning, a streak of dark black smoke rising into the afternoon sky.

"Holy shit, look at this," Paul says.

"That's where we just came from," Matt says. "They're destroying the evidence, man. That's the truck with all the gold in it," he continues.

"That's diesel fuel, man," Paul says.

"Look, we have the evidence we need and it's very important we don't lose it. There's nothing we can do about that now. We need to roll out," Matt says.

Paul and Matt drive away and exit the Pine Barrens as the cloud of smoke reaches higher and higher. The truck they have found earlier is now burning, destroying its contents and everything else. The truck sparks one final time before it tips over and explodes in a massive fireball.

Chapter 11

November 2017, 10:00 a.m.

He knew he was in trouble. He knew his world would soon come crashing down around him. Chris Reed sits at his desk with his Glock pistol in hand. He swipes everything off in a fit of rage as he places his pistol against his right temple. He shuts his eyes as he pulls the trigger but his gun won't fire but instead jams. Chris sits back down in his chair and realizes he still has a little more time on his hands, but knows that his whistle-blower friends are watching their every move. They're not as easy to capture unlike the previous people that have attempted the same. Chris fixes the jam in his pistol and fires one shot into the wall. He then heads toward the window as the rain comes down heavily and stares out before running out of his office angrier than a bull.

Back in Manhattan, Paul and Matt wait impatiently for Amanda to arrive in the pouring rain.

"What's taking her so long?" Matt asks as he paces around the room.

"She'll get here don't worry," Paul responds. At that moment, the doorbell rings. "Speak of the devil," Paul says getting off the couch to answer the door. Paul answers the door and let's Amanda in after a long wait.

"Sorry, I'm late. I hit traffic along with this lousy weather," Amanda says after kissing Paul.

"Well, I can't blame you," Paul jokes. "Here, I'll take your coat," he continues.

"Boy, do we have a lot to tell you," Matt says.

"Yes, that's why I came here today, and I have a lot to share too," Amanda implies.

"Well, let's get started here. Matt and I found something incredible a few weeks ago," Paul says, turning his laptop on.

Paul opens up the file which shows the photos of the abandoned truck carrying the gold bullion from the towers he snapped. Amanda is aghast at what she sees.

"So that gold rumor was true all along. I thought that was a myth," Amanda says in shock.

"It was no myth. That gold isn't even from the United States, it's from Saudi Arabia," Matt explains.

"I remember something that you guys should know. Congress tried to investigate this heist and was almost shutdown by the Coleman White House at the time. One member of congress even went missing, a republican from New Jersey trying to find it himself," Amanda explains. Paul and Matt get chills after hearing Amanda's new information.

"I remember the media went nuts over that, wall-to-wall coverage nonstop for the next week or so," Paul explains.

"Did they find him?" Matt asks.

"I don't know, but I do know that someone did fill his seat a few days later, a democrat," Amanda says.

"So, he could still be alive somewhere," Matt implies.

"I wouldn't put my money on it," Paul says.

At that moment, the storm outside knocks out the power to the apartment plunging them into darkness. Paul's laptop is wireless and thus stays on but loses its connection to the internet.

"Goddamn it," Paul says, getting up. "You've got to be kidding," he continues.

"Why isn't the backup generator kicking in?" Matt asks.

"I don't know. I'll go check," Paul says running to the back of his apartment. He finds out that his generator has been disconnected by someone before the storm started. He heads back into the living room to tell the others.

"Bad news, I'm going to have to call an electrician because that generator's been mysteriously disconnected," Paul explains.

"We're stuck with no electric for a while," he continues. At the precise moment, Amanda's cell phone rings.

"Hello," she answers.

All they hear is the constant falling of the heavy rain right outside their window.

"Hello, whoever you are, this isn't funny," Amanda says, getting angry.

Paul grabs the phone out of Amanda's hand to try to see who's on the other end of the line. "Listen closely, you motherfucker, I'm going to call the cops if you don't quit fucking around!" Paul shouts into the phone.

"You three are in grave danger." The voice laughs before the call cuts out.

Amanda gets a series of chills after hearing the voice on the other end of the phone. "Oh my god, no, please no," she says starting to panic.

"You need to calm down," Paul says. "It could be a prank call," he continues.

"Did you take a stupid pill earlier? This is no prank, think about it. Matt's wife was kidnapped and almost killed forcing her into witness protection for fuck's sake," Amanda explains. "I believe we are in grave danger, and there's nothing we can do about it," she continues.

"Yes, there is something we can do. Get those thoughts out of your head and don't let it drag you down," Paul says. "I said this to you earlier at the memorial," he continues. "If we let those thoughts drag us down, we're finished and it'll tear us apart and we want to succeed not blow it at the last moment," Matt explains.

"Exactly, now you're thinking the right way," Paul says.

Finally, the power is restored to the apartment after a long couple of minutes.

"It's about time that happened," Matt says. "Now we can discuss what we were supposed to be talking about," he continues.

Paul reboots his laptop and pops up the same series of images he had on before. "What was this congressman's name?" Paul asks Amanda.

"I believe it was Ron Forrestal," she replies.

Paul types in the name and gets the congressman's biography. "Ronald D. Forrestal, born August 23, 1948. Disappeared May 11, 2004, in New Jersey," Paul reads. "A Republican first elected to congress in 1976, ran for president in 2000 and lost to James Coleman, married with three children," Paul continues.

"He disappeared on May 11, 2004, after trying to find the gold bullion trucks after his investigation in congress was nearly shutdown," Paul says as he gets an adrenaline rush. "Listen to this, it says that Forrestal was a huge critic of Coleman's intentions to go to war in the Middle East and wanted a new investigation of what happened at the towers," Paul reads.

"We all know that Coleman orchestrated the whole thing," Amanda says.

"Yes, that part we get, but it's possible that Coleman or somebody close to him wanted to get rid of Forrestal because he would be a threat to him," Matt explains.

"That makes a lot of sense when you think about it," Paul says. "Here's the problem, we don't know if he's still alive or dead," Paul continues.

"I told you that earlier," Amanda says.

"Well, I'll tell you this, we didn't find him in the Pine Barrens which is probably where he would most likely be," Paul says.

"Look, I think he's probably dead and we have other things to do," Matt says.

"Right, but just know this, we've come a long way in exposing the truth and we won't rest until we do," Paul says grinning.

That night, the storm outside has since died down as Paul gets ready to turn in. He makes himself a peanut butter and jelly sandwich before he heads to bed. He turns off the television and his desk lamp and slowly tries to fall asleep. As he does so, he imagines himself back at Windows on the World in 2001 at his cousin's wedding.

Everything was normal until the fire alarms start going off one by one.

"Hey, what the hell is happening?" Paul asks.

"I don't know, sir, we'll go check," one of the many waiters says.

He goes to check on the problem only to be engulfed in a giant wall of flames. The flames reach the main ballroom where the party takes place.

"Paul, help me please!" his mother shouts.

Paul rushes over to where his mother is on the floor trying to put out the flames on her jacket.

"What's happening?" he asks, getting emotional.

At that moment, several of the windows shatter sending a cascade of glass in every direction. Paul hears the sound of dozens of fire trucks on the streets below. The restaurant burns around him as he watches hundreds of guests panic trying to save themselves. Finally, something knocks Paul out the window causing him to plunge 107 stories to his death.

"We've got jumpers coming down!" a firefighter's radio says.

Paul wakes up sweating like crazy as he checks the clock on his nightstand. It's only eleven at night. He's only slept an hour. Another horrible nightmare rocks him to his core. Paul believes his nightmares are a sign of things to come, things he can't even begin to imagine.

A few days later, Amanda is sitting down doing more research on her laptop computer. She finds something that really gets her attention. She finds out about a secret military bunker from the Cold War that was built underneath the Twin Towers in the seventies. She read on and finds out that the secret bunker was used as a storage area for yellowcake uranium rods for nuclear power. The uranium was since removed in the late nineties and shipped to a nuclear waste dump in New Mexico. Before the rods were placed there, the CIA used it as a secret torture chamber for foreign agents and was used as a secret human trafficking ring. The bunker was destroyed when both towers collapsed on top of it. Amanda proceeds to print out the article to show Paul when they meet again at Central Park. An hour later, Paul meets Amanda at Central Park for lunch.

"I understand you wanted to show me something, correct?" he asks, sitting down.

"Yes, I do," Amanda says handing him the article. "It seems as if Coleman wasn't the only one to have a motive to destroy the towers," she continues.

"This talks about human trafficking done by the CIA underneath the buildings," Paul reads.

"Keep reading," she says.

"It says this happened in the eighties, along with cruel and unusual punishment for foreign spies," he reads on.

"Don't forget about the yellowcake uranium that was stored there," Amanda says.

"Wait a second. I see what's happening here. The CIA wanted to destroy all this. After all, their records showed no evidence of this," Paul explains.

"Well, succeeded in doing so, the towers fell right on top of it. So we have Coleman who did this for money and popularity, and now the CIA for obstruction of justice," Amanda explains.

"Nobody has uncovered stuff like this until now," Paul says.

"Well, remember others have tried and have failed but we might succeed," Amanda says.

Paul spots a few people staring at him on a park bench a few feet away from him. "Look over there," he tells Amanda.

She looks over her shoulder and sees two guys in black suits heading toward them.

"We need to get out of here now," Paul says. "Don't lose that article, I think that's what they want," he continues. The two hightail it out of Central Park with the two mysterious men right behind them. Paul takes out his pistol and fires one shot and misses as the bullet ricochets off a tree. Numerous people in the area start to panic and scream running in fear.

The two men manage to fire off a couple of rounds themselves and also miss. Paul and Amanda manage to make it to the car but are shocked when it explodes in front of them into pieces.

"My car!" Paul shouts. "Goddamn it, this way!" he shouts again.

Paul and Amanda duck behind a series of tall shrubs and watch and listen carefully. Paul reloads his pistol just in case they get jumped.

"Where'd they go?" one of the men asks.

"Keep looking, they won't get very far," his partner replies.

"What the fuck is going on here?" Amanda asks whispering in Paul's ear.

"I don't know, sweetie, but it doesn't look good. I think they want our heads on platters," Paul explains. The two men approach the tall shrub Paul and Amanda are currently hiding behind. One of them pulls the shrub back, only to reveal nothing but solid pavement.

"Fuck!" the man shouts. "Find them now damn it!" he continues.

Paul and Amanda exited Central Park before the two mysterious men even knew where to look.

"I think I know where they're headed," one of the men says as they walk away.

Meanwhile, at the state department in DC, Vice President Richards decides to have a little talk with Secretary Rich Abens. Abens is fifty-five years of age, has smooth brown hair with a trimmed beard and mustache, has green eyes, and is five foot nine.

"Mr. Vice President, glad you could make it today at the department of state," Abens says with excitement.

"Sit down, Rich," Richards says.

"What is it, sir, everything okay?" Abens asks.

"No, it's not okay!" Richards shouts.

"Sir, what's going on here?" Abens asks again.

"I received a highly classified folder which details the events of who really brought down the World Trade Center back in 2001, and your name is in it!" Richards shouts.

"Sir, that was a horrible tragedy that we will never forget as a country," Abens says.

"Yeah, a horrible tragedy that you and former president Coleman planned, and you know what really makes me sick to my stomach is that you watched the whole thing from a balcony while partying!" Richards says, slamming his fists down. "I guess you were really excited about getting a small fraction of that money, weren't you, Mr. Secretary?" Richards questions.

"What party?" Abens asks, clenching his teeth.

Vice President Richards takes out the picture of Abens, before he became secretary of state, watching the events from an apartment balcony with a beer in hand. "Look familiar at all to you?" Richards asks.

Abens starts to get anxious as he knows something is up. His blood pressure starts to rise as he starts to sweat. "Where'd you find this?" Abens asks.

"That's for me to know and for you to wonder," Richards whispers into Abens' face.

"I've worked for this department for most of my adult life Mr. Vice President, and I've been waiting to be named secretary and I can't believe you'd tarnish my reputation," Abens says angrily. "I was thinking of leaving at the beginning of next year, but now I might want to leave a little earlier," Abens continues.

"Why? So you can flee the country and get away with everything?" Richards questions. "You see, Mr. Secretary, I'm one small step ahead of you," Richards whispers. "We'll see what Mike has to say about all this later on," he continues. "I swore you into this office and thought you'd be loyal, but we found out that you wanted half of the money from the Middle East for your involvement!" he shouts before leaving.

Richards leaves the state department as Abens is overcome with anger and anxiety. He throws his chair against the wall and watches it break into pieces.

Meanwhile, President Atlas calls Defense secretary Newman into the Oval Office. "Mr. Newman, please sit down," Atlas says.

"Sir, you'd be happy to know that we've received intelligence of a secret Syrian nuclear program," Newman explains.

"Excellent, but that's not why I called you here today, that news can wait," Atlas says.

"Sir, this news is important," Newman implies.

"Let's discuss other things first. You see, the vice president and I came into possession of a top-secret classified folder no other government official has ever seen before. It talks about the destruction of the Twin Towers back in '01," Atlas explains.

Newman feels a rush of anger run through him. "The folder," he whispers to himself.

"Now, I want to talk about your involvement in the biggest attack on US soil!" Atlas shouts.

"Sir?" Newman questions.

"Don't play dumb, Newman, your fingerprints are all over this!" Atlas shouts again.

"I don't know what you're talking about," Newman says.

"You were a buddy with former president Coleman, is that right?" Atlas questions.

"I was a defense contractor when he was president so yes we were friends," Newman explains.

"Did he ask you to deplete nearly 2.3 billion dollars from the department's bank account?" Atlas questions.

"No he didn't," Newman reluctantly says.

"That's the wrong answer. You know what Newman? I don't like liars and I never did my whole life. That 2.3 billion you drained from the Pentagon was used to destroy two skyscrapers in Lower Manhattan!" the president shouts.

Newman doesn't say a single word as his anger builds; he knows he's in trouble.

"I knew you'd say nothing," Atlas says.

Newman gets up and prepares to leave. "This stuff isn't true and I'm not going to take it. Here's the info on the Syrian nuclear program," Newman says as he walks out.

"This isn't over, Newman. I'm going to get to the bottom of this. I know you're guilty!" Atlas shouts.

As Newman leaves the Oval Office, he vows he will never get caught as his blood boils faster than a pot of water on the stove. He gets on his phone and calls James Coleman. "James, they're on to me. I'm coming down," Newman says angrily.

Both Atlas and Richards know that soon the truth will be revealed faster than anyone can predict.

Later that night, heavy rain pounds the area. At the Federation headquarters, Chris Reed sits in a small interrogation room as he thinks to himself. He hears the rain coming down outside the room which only fuels his anger. He walks out of the room for a split second and stares at a picture of himself alongside Coleman from 2001.

"This is your problem now," Reed whispers.

He heads back into the room and pulls out a Remington 870 shotgun from underneath the large metal table. He sits in the corner and cocks the shotgun and puts one round into the chamber. He puts the tip of the gun in his mouth as a stray tear comes down his left eye before he closes them both and pulls the trigger, blowing a huge hole in the back of his head. Coleman and Browning hear the mysterious sound from the lobby and head up to investigate. They discover Reed's body in the interrogation room, dead of an apparent suicide.

"Goddamn it!" Coleman shouts. "This was our last hope. This means we're fucked, Nick!" he continues.

"We need to leave now," Browning says.

Chapter 12

January 4, 2018, 10:00 a.m.

President Atlas returns from his holiday vacation and wants to start his second year in office on a high note. As he does so, he notices something is up. He's talked to several of his cabinet secretaries over the holiday vacation and they have all assured him the allegations against them are false. The president also notices that some haven't been showing up to meetings. Their deputies attend instead. Most notably, Rich Abens and Eric Newman have been awfully quiet ever since their interrogation a few months ago. He knows that his cabinet is in a crisis, but it doesn't affect his job as president. He'll have to let them go at some point and replace them with more effective leaders that are loyal. Now, as Vice President Richards enters the Oval Office, they begin taking about the strange behavior they've been seeing.

"Sir, have you noticed that Abens and Newman have been absent from recent meetings?" Richards asks.

"Yes, I have, Rich. It's really strange and I think I know what's going on here," Atlas says. "You showed me the evidence against them, and it's very damaging to them. Newman depleted the Pentagon's bank account to fund the effort to destroy the towers, while Abens wanted half of all the money once the job was done," he explains.

"I think they're planning to flee the country," Richards says.

"Well, then we have a job to do and we will stop them," Atlas says, sitting down.

Back in New York City, Paul is finally ready to open up to his mother about what he's been doing for the last year. He last saw his mother, Sabrina, over the holiday at her new apartment in Staten Island where she resettled after the attacks took place. Things have long since change with Sabrina. She's sixty-nine years old now and in failing health, but that won't stop her son from telling the truth.

"I'm glad you decided to give me a call after visiting me, son," Sabrina says.

"Look, Mom, I need to tell you something important," Paul says.

"You can tell me anything," she says.

"For the past year, I've always known my former agency was hiding something, and I finally have the evidence to prove that they destroyed the World Trade Center with the help of former president Coleman to enrich themselves in foreign money and to boost his popularity among his base," Paul explains.

"Son, this is pure fantasy and I don't want to leave this world knowing you have lost your mind with rumors from the internet," his mother explains.

"Mom, you have to believe me here. People have been chasing and hunting me down for this, which means I'm right," Paul says.

"Son, what happened to you? Now you know why the family won't talk to you as much. Your father died in 2015 and he'd be pretty disappointed in you right now," Sabrina implies. "I have to go now son," she continues.

"Mom, please don't hang up. I love you," Paul says getting emotional.

"I love you too, son, we'll talk soon," his mother says before hanging up.

Paul starts crying as he collapses onto the floor as he fears he'll never speak to his family again. Matt's wife, Anne, isn't talking to him either. She just wants the whole thing to end so their life can continue. Every time he calls, he just gets her voicemail. Their families want no part in whatever they have uncovered. Paul and Matt are on their own for the time being. Isolated and alone, they're running out of time. Now Matt calls his friend as he gets hit with a wave of anxiety.

"Bro, I can't take it anymore. Anne won't talk to me," Matt says.

"It's the same thing with me, man. My mother just told me that my family is cutting ties with me," Paul says composing himself.

"That's horrible, so what do we do?" Matt asks.

"You're going to have to let it play out. I don't think it'll last long," Paul says. "Look, I'll be at your place in about ten minutes," he continues.

As Paul gets ready to head to his friend's apartment, Amanda wraps up her early lunch at a friend's house. Her friend was a former FBI agent who claims to have info regarding the disappearance of Congressman Ron Forrestal. The man claims that Forrestal was abducted by other FBI agents and executed in a remote area to silence him about a possible new investigation into the towers' destruction.

"This is one hell of a bombshell," Amanda says.

"I've worked for the FBI for twenty years and I have never seen anything like it in my life," the former agent says. "It's very important you don't lose this. People have been after me for years regarding this find," he continues. "I won't sir, and thank you very much," Amanda says, heading out the door. She gets in her car and puts the important information in her purse pocket. She then proceeds to drive away from the agent's home. As she drives away, her car starts to act strangely.

It starts to build up a tremendous amount speed. Amanda is no longer in control of her own car.

"What's going on? I can't control it!" she shouts.

She looks at her speed which is now over 40 miles per hour in a twenty mph zone. She has little time to react as her car is heading toward a guardrail. She undoes her seatbelt, takes her purse, and manages to roll out of the car, scraping her right leg and arm in the process. She watches in horror as the car crashes through the guardrail and explodes.

"Help me! Help me!" she shouts. Amanda gets the attention of a police officer who saw the whole thing from a nearby intersection.

"Ma'am you okay?" the officer asks. "Let's get you up," he says.

"I don't know what just happened here officer," Amanda says in shock.

"Ma'am you're going to have to come with me and answer some questions," the officer says.

"You serious?" she asks.

"Ma'am you were going too fast on a residential street. What we're you thinking?" the officer asks.

"I wasn't thinking anything. I wasn't even in control, it was completely unresponsive," Amanda explains.

"Yeah, you need to come down now," the cop says. "We'll patch up your injuries and then ask you about your reckless driving okay," he continues.

"Sir, I used to work for the US government you know," Amanda says.

"Doesn't matter, you think that's going to get you out of this, keep dreaming," the officer replies as he handcuffs her. "You'll be fine," he continues. "I will say you are looking at a year in jail for this, now I'm not saying you will but we have to investigate and I have to go through the scenarios," he goes on to say before he escorts Amanda to the station.

Meanwhile, on the other side of the city, a team of three masked men break a padlocked gate to an abandoned shipyard rumored to house one of the last pieces of steel from the towers, originally intended to be shipped to a scrap yard in China to be melted down and turned into new building material for the communist country's naval program.

The project was cancelled in 2002 after the shipyard closed due to bankruptcy amid government interference. The team of three are former Navy SEALs lead by their leader who goes by the nickname of "Rough." They enter the shipyard and head to a small bridge where rough takes out a pair of binoculars.

"There it is," he says. Rough also carries a body camera which sends a signal to a laptop computer where Paul and Matt watch the live feed from their apartment.

"Are you getting all this, Mitchell?" Rough asks.

"Yes, I am, now keep moving," he replies through the microphone.

"You got it. Let's move!" Rough shouts. They begin their journey to one of many abandoned freighters as a security camera records their every move. They eventually make it to the freighter carrying the last remnant of the World Trade Center. On board, they finally see the steel beam. A huge piece from the foundation of the north tower chained to the rusted deck of a decomposing vessel.

Rough spots a piece of paper underneath the beam and picks it up and proceeds to read it.

"What's it read rough?" Paul asks into the microphone.

"It's a scrapping order signed by FEMA after it was inspected for explosive residue which came back negative," Rough explains.

"That's a lie. Explosive residue was found on numerous pieces. I'm sure that one has residue as well," Paul says.

At that moment, the feed cuts out and Paul and Matt lose contact with their three men.

"What the hell? Get them back now!" Matt shouts.

"I'm trying, man, I can't reestablish contact," Paul says.

"You've got to keep trying!" Matt shouts.

Back on the ship, the men don't realize their contact has been cut.

"Mitchell, are you there? Come in Mitchell, over!" Rough shouts. "How about you Pierce?" he asks.

No answer, instead only static white noise. Rough turns to his men and begins to suspect something sinister is taking place.

"I think someone's fucking with us," he says.

One of them turns around and spots a group of men boarding the vessel. "We think you're right, look," one of the men says.

A few minutes later, Paul reestablishes contact but notices the body camera is now on the deck of the ship.

"Matt, get over here something's wrong!" Paul shouts.

"What is it?" he asks. "I can't get any sound," Paul says. Unexpectedly, a body slams down on the deck with blood running from the mouth along with the eyes wide-open. The camera then shows the face of a government agent out to get blood.

"We're coming for you," he whispers into the camera before cutting out.

Matt slams the laptop closed and starts pacing around the room. They know something is deeply wrong. Both can feel the anxiety rushing through them. There's nothing they can do at this point except wait for the release of the folder. What they aren't aware of is that it's slowly starting to unravel day by day. A few hours later, after treating her injuries, Amanda arrives at the police station for questioning. They let her place one phone call out before they ask the questions. She calls Paul.

"Hi, honey," she says emotionally.

"Amanda, where the fuck have you been? I've been trying to reach you all day," Paul asks.

"I'm in a little situation right now. I'm at the police station," Amanda says.

"What?" Paul asks.

"They're going to ask me about my supposed reckless driving," she replies.

"Oh goddamn it, Amanda, what the hell?" Paul asks, getting emotional.

"I didn't do anything. I lost control of my car," she says. "I need you to come and get me out," she continues.

"Wrap it up," the officer says.

"I got to go," she says. Amanda is then brought into a small room where the questioning begins.

"Okay, Ms. Knox, tell me everything that happened," the officer says.

"Well, I was coming home from a friend's house and I don't know, I just lost control of my car. It felt like someone else was driving," she explains. "I believe it was hacked," she continues.

"Who is this friend you speak of?" the officer asks.

"He used to be in the FBI and he gave me some important information. After all, I used to work for the government," she explains.

"What info did he give you?" the officer asks.

"He gave me info regarding the disappearance of Congressman Ron Forrestal. My friends and I believe he was murdered for trying to start a new investigation into the destruction of the World Trade Center. I have it with me if you want it," Amanda says. "I believe someone hacked my car to try and get rid of me," she continues.

"Ms. Knox, no such technology exists. Why can't you just admit you drove recklessly because you are intoxicated?" the officer asks.

"What I'm saying is true, sir," she says.

"In regards to this Forrestal guy you speak of, I think you're living in the Land of Oz and the wizard isn't home, sweetheart," the officer says. "You're going to sit there and tell me that my friends who I knew very well were killed by our own government? All twenty-three of them!" the officer shouts. "If you're going to peddle bullshit like that, then you should be isolated from society!" he continues. "I was there and saw it all unfold. My friends entered those buildings and never came home! Where the hell were you?" he asks angrily.

Amanda sat silently trying to hold back her emotions after bringing up what she's been doing. "I've heard enough for one day," he says. "Guard!" he shouts. "Take her away," he says.

"This isn't fair, Officer. What I'm saying is true. Believe me, please!" Amanda shouts as she's escorted out of the room.

As night falls over, DC secretary of state Rich Abens and Defense secretary Eric Newman meet at an undisclosed location near Foggy Bottom. Abens watches as Newman's motorcade arrives at the area where they shake each other's hands before heading inside.

"You know why I called you here tonight, right Eric?" Abens asks.

"Yes, I do," he whispers.

"We've been discussing this for quite some time now, and here it is," Abens says, walking over to retrieve the items. "Here they are, sir," Abens continues as he hands Newman the items.

"Our passports, they're finished," Newman says.

"Yes, they are, sir," Abens says excitedly.

"Atlas knows everything. We're finished you know. We'll never make it to Europe," Newman says anxiously.

"Never say never, Mr. Newman. You should be glad we're doing this. After all, that money did me some good after those towers fell," Abens explains.

"Atlas is coming back from Ohio soon," Newman says. "We failed to keep this secret, I mean us blowing up the two biggest buildings in New York City just to enrich ourselves along with boosting Coleman's popularity," he continues.

"I busted my ass for these passports, Newman, and you're going where I'm going!" Abens shouts.

"I know that already. I can't believe it ends right here," Newman says. "This is all Crawford's fault. If he hadn't given that damn folder to those three mother fuckers, we wouldn't be in this mess!" he shouts.

"Now you see why we had to get rid of him, don't you?" Abens asks.

"Yes, I do," Newman says.

"In just a few short hours, we'll be headed to Europe to live the rest of our lives in peace. We have no choice. That folder is our death sentence and we won't be here when this happens," Abens says.

Their conversation is interrupted by the sound of Marine One and its decoy about to land at the White House.

"He's come back, Rich, we need to go now," Newman says.

"Let's go," Abens says.

Back in New York City, Paul and Matt head to the station to pick up Amanda after learning of her arrest a few hours earlier.

"I can't fucking believe this. We were on the cusp of revealing the biggest secret in the history of the country, and Amanda gets arrested for supposed reckless driving!" Paul shouts with his teeth clenched together.

"Relax, man, it'll be fine," Matt says.

"No, it's not going to be fine. They got her," Paul says.

"You're saying the government set her up to get arrested," Matt implies.

"Bingo, you hit the nail on the goddamn head," he says angrily. "I didn't want to do this tonight, man. I really didn't," he continues.

"Look, just relax, man," Matt says.

"I think we might succeed here," Paul says with confidence.

"I hope the president reads this. It would be a huge slap in the fucking face if he didn't," Matt says. "We worked our ass off since last May to do this and we finally did it," he continues.

At that moment, they're stopped when a series of bright head-lights turn on, revealing several trucks along with a team of men with guns drawn.

"What the fuck is this?" Paul asks angrily. The two look at each other and believe they know the answer to what they're both seeing in front of them.

"Paul Mitchell and Matthew Pierce, come out the car with your hands above your heads now!" one of the many officers says.

They decline to come out and still try to comprehend the situation.

"If you don't come out, we'll shoot!" they say.

"Let's get this over with. There's nothing we can do," Paul says.

With that, both men get out of the car as the team of agents proceed to handcuff both of them while taking their firearms away and unloading them. A black sack is placed over both their heads before they are pistol-whipped, practically knocking them uncon-scious. They are then placed into two separate trucks while another agent proceeds to drive Paul's car. The trucks then drive away from the area with the full moon shinning overhead.

In the meantime, Marine One touches down on the South Lawn of the White House. President Atlas salutes his Marine guard as he steps off his helicopter where the folder that Vice President Richards has been reading and that he was briefed on now sits on the resolute desk waiting his approval for release.

About the Author

Paul Antonucci was born, raised, and still lives on Long Island, New York. His interests include but are not limited to, US history, government, and politics. He writes about many different genres such as thrillers/suspense, horror, mystery, historical fiction, postapocalyptic. Even though he has been writing for a while, this is his first published work. In his free time, he enjoys amateur filmmaking, computer programing, and spectator sports.

CPSIA information can be obtained
at www.ICGtesting.com
Printed in the USA
LVHW091209210819
628263LV00024B/372/P